Scents Of A Woman

Kwame Ronnie Vanderhorst

•

Typestyles Times Roman, Harrington

•

ISBN 0-9652104-5-6

HOTEP PRODUCTIONS
© 1999

To book Kwame Ronnie Vanderhorst or for additional information to
order his books, tapes and materials, contact:
Prepare Our Youth, Inc.
6856 Eastern Avenue NW Suite 207
Washington, D.C. 20012
(202) 291-5040 (202) 291-5042 fax
Web Site: www.poyinc.org

Dedicated

To the women of
Emmanuel - Brinklow,
whose lovely 'scents'
pervaded our home,
hearts and spirits during my wife's illness.
May our Creator grant
you health, peace and
blessings.

Sincerely,
Kwame

Acknowledgments

Onyamee Kwame, The Creator

Stevan Vanderhorst

Jomo Howard Bullard

Jean R. Baker

Patrick Thomas

Althea Ramsammy

Eugene & Beverly Broady

Joyce Tapscott

William Hoover

Timekee Turner

Kenneth Anderson

Angela Davis

Mac Claxton

Andrea Chapman

Eddie Curry

Ralph & Brenda Jones

In His Name Ministries

Prepare Our Youth supporters

Table of Contents

Introduction

Scents Of A Woman is the female companion to my book, *Smellin' Ourselves: What Men Need To Understand About Ourselves and Our Women.*

This book is not tit-for-tat, that is, I wrote a book for men; now I am obligated to write a book for women. I'm not trying to even the score. I truly have some musings in my spirit that I want to share with women concerning their relationships with men.

In our Creator's divine plan for human existence, man was not complete until woman was created. In this, and no other relationship, can human procreation, progeny, or society exist or continue. There is no so-called alternate lifestyle that can accomplish this fact. The male-female relationship is the most complementary natural order of human existence. Male-female relationships are the highest expression of our Creator's oneness on earth.

In my attempt to characterize or categorize women, flowers are the imagery that comes to my mind. My research has rewarded me with an amazing discovery of the similarities between women and flowers. Both are beautiful and delicate, diverse in color and sensual in ambience. Like enchanting flowers, women are captivating and fascinating.

Although women are similar in many respects, like flowers, they are also different and unique. Each woman has her distinctive qualities. Like varied fragrances of flowers, there are *scents* of a woman. Experiences and encounters bring the scents of a woman to the fore. Yet, amid the scents of a woman, there is usually a predominant scent. This *scent* cannot be veiled or hidden.

When a man interacts with a woman, usually, he will

encounter her scent. Comparable to a cheap or costly perfume, a man inhales a woman's scent. And like a flower, a woman's scent either attracts or repels. Her scent inhibits or enhances her male-female relationships.

There are scents of a woman that enhance male-female relationships, scents such as, self-control, kindness, tact, integrity and flexibility, to name a few. These enhancing scents are not manufactured for the moment. These scents of a woman have been carefully cultivated long before womanhood.

Conversely, there are scents of a woman that drive men crazy! These not-so-positive scents of a woman elicit a myriad of reactions from men. These scents irritate, exasperate, nauseate, infuriate, and even alienate men from their women and relationships.

There are certain scents women exude into the atmosphere of male-female relationships that inhibit its growth and maturation, challenging its stability and oftentimes, weakening their man's total commitment to them and their relationship.

For instance, there is a man I'm familiar with whose wife is sexually involved with another man. She is not even discreet about it, although discretion never excuses wrongdoing. Her scents of belligerence and indifference are literally driving her husband crazy! He is at the point of a nervous breakdown! She could care less!

All women have scents that may inhibit or enhance. As I previously mentioned, each woman emanates a predominant scent above her other scents. **The predominant scent of a woman is actually the SPIRIT of a woman, the activating or essential principle of her whole being.**

In my desire for balance, I address scents of a woman that inhibit male-female relationships from experiencing mutual fulfillment. I also share scents of a woman that enhance male-female relationships, keeping the relationship growing, maturing, exciting, and productive! These scents inspire most men to be faithful and totally committed to their women and family.

Although the enhancing scents of a woman cannot guarantee that all men will be faithful and committed, enhancing scents are part of the solution in the quest for mutually-fulfilling male-female relationships.

• ***Scents Of A Woman*** is the female counterpart to my book, Smellin' Ourselves: What Men Need To Understand About Ourselves And Our Women. (You must read both books to see how they complement each other).

• ***Scents Of A Woman*** encourage parents to sow and cultivate specific seeds in girls and young ladies that will blossom to enhance male-female relationships.

• ***Scents Of A Woman*** inspires women to acknowledge inhibiting growths and formations in their spirit that need careful but necessary pruning.

• ***Scents Of A Woman*** urges women to seek principled solutions, bring closure to a painful past, and blossom anew into a glorious future.

• ***Scents Of A Woman*** offers refreshing, sweet-smelling scents that permeate the atmosphere of male-female relationships, parenting and family.

Defining Moments

I buy my wife perfume. It takes me a while to find the right perfume. I want more than the right fragrance. I want a perfume that complements her personality, her style, her ambience, her *spirit.*

But of all the perfumes I have given her, there is no perfume that could duplicate her true essence - her scent. I wish I could reproduce her scent, put it into a bottle, and give it to every woman who needs to replace their inhibiting scents in male-female relationships with my wife's enhancing scent.

Every woman has defining moments when her scent, her predominant spirit, becomes readily noticeable. My wife's defining moment came as we sat in the physician's office as he gave us results of her biopsy of a small lump right above her right breast. "Mrs. Vanderhorst, you have cancer."

I watched my wife bow her head. A tear trickled down her beautiful, ebony face. I sat there stunned and silent. Later that day, I asked her what was going on with her at that moment the physician said, "cancer." She said, "I was choosing my attitude, and it will be an attitude of praise! I'm going to praise my way healed!"

My wife, who is deeply spiritual, made a conscious decision that she would praise our Creator, even in the midst of her uncertain future. This experience has been the most profound defining moment in her personal life, as well as our marriage and family. Although I have always maintained the utmost love and respect for my wife, and held her in my highest regard, this experience has indubitably heightened my esteem for her.

Not once did she complain, even during her grueling treatments. She has maintained a poise and dignity that defies reason. Breast cancer is no joke! Not only does it invade a woman's body, it can assail her soul and spirit like a relentless stalker.

It is said, "Crisis and challenges don't make character; they reveal character." It was as if a new, refreshing, sweet-smelling scent was uncapped, that had been sealed within my wife until this defining moment. The mellifluous scent she released into the atmosphere of our marriage and family cannot be bottled or sold. It can only be experienced!

The spirit of peace she exuded was so profound that my eldest daughter wrote a note to her saying, "Mommy, your peace has given me peace." Her note, more than anything else, gave witness to my wife's enhancing spirit during her illness and subsequent treatment.

When my wife and I first told our two daughters that their mother had cancer, they asked two questions: "Are you going to die?" and, "Are we going to get cancer?" It can be a disturbing time in a child's life when an experience of this magnitude hits home. But my wife, though broad-sided by the ominous news of cancer, comparable to a crushed flower, gave off such an enhancing scent that our daughters didn't despair, but actually excelled.

A month or so later, our eldest daughter was inducted into the National Honor Society. Six months later, our youngest daughter graduated from the eighth grade as salutatorian, having all A's, with the exception of two B's all year! Our Creator be praised!

When you combine the enhancing spirit of a woman and the right spirit of a man, you have heaven on earth!

Many women have not taken catastrophic news or painful experiences, be it personal or in their male-female relationships, with such nobility and resolve as my wife. I have seen women whose defining moment came during divorce. One woman I know, reeks with the foul scents of anger and revenge. This woman's spirit is so toxic that she may end up physically sick. This woman, like so many others, becomes unpleasant to be around. Her spirit now repels those who once enjoyed being in her company.

Another woman I know emanates the extraordinary scents of tact and grace in response to her painful divorce. She never speaks against her former spouse, not even to her two sons. She never whines or accuses. Her spirit exudes a quiet faith and confidence in our Creator, which was readily evident to all who know her. Her sons are doing very well, although they wish their parents were still together. Her spirit during this defining moment has made the difference, not only for her sons, but also for her own well-being.

I understand why there is a diversity of scents of a woman. The scents of a woman are not produced on the spot. Scents are a gradual blend of a female's upbringing, relationships, experiences and encounters which, during defining moments, certainly reveal her predominant spirit.

Like the growth of a flower, I call a female's upbringing, **sowing**, and her relationships, experiences and encounters, **pollinating**.

Although each female's sowing and pollinating process may differ, the principles of the seeds and flowers never change. In short, a woman reaps what has been sown in her by her upbringing.

Most plants pass on life to future plant generations by seeds. It is the work of a flower to make seed. Flowering plants make new plants by means of seeds. Inside the plant's seed is a baby plant called the embryo. In the ground, under the right conditions of warmth and moisture, the embryo begins to grow. It breaks out of the seed coat and pushes up through the soil into the sunshine. It develops into a plant that in turn will produce new seeds.

When the seeds are ripe, they must leave the parent plant. Every seed has some way of traveling. Some may travel only a few inches. Others may travel many miles. If all seeds fell to the ground directly beneath the parent plant, they would be too crowded and too shaded to grow. They must find good soil and plenty of space and sunshine if they are to develop into strong, healthy plants.

Other plants break loose from the soil in the autumn and roll with the wind, scattering their seeds over the countryside. Such plants are called tumbleweeds.[1]

[1] Microsoft Encarta 97 Encyclopedia

Sowing

Parenting is sowing. The embryo is formed within the mother, and under the right conditions, this embryo begins to grow. Growth begins immediately. What parents sow or fail to sow within a female either enhances or inhibits the growth and development of their daughter.

Unfortunately, some parents are not as attentive to prenatal details, and through the use of drugs, alcohol, nicotine and other harmful choices, the embryo and its growth are adversely affected.

Conscientious parents take into account the fact that their daughter may one day produce *seed* of her own, therefore, the sowing process should not be underestimated. The sowing a female receives as a child and youth will ultimately affect her own seed.

Although the environment and other variables may affect the seed, it is the parents or guardians of females who play a prominent role in the sowing of seeds. Even if a parent is not there for her, for whatever reason, that is still a seed sown.

It is incumbent upon parents to provide the most conducive home environment they possibly can for sowing. But no external accouterments, no matter how opulent, can ever substitute for the right seeds sown in female character development and its inevitable growth process.

As I mentioned in my book, *Smellin' Ourselves: What Men Need To Understand About Ourselves And Our Women,* if a girl's parents are separated or divorced, when a father understands that he is to protect his daughter's spirit, he will be positively involved and assiduously supportive in his daughter's growth and maturation process.

A father's willing cooperation with his daughter's mother is quintessential in his daughter gaining a healthy perspective of males. Later in the book, we will see what may happen when a father is not cooperative, involved or supportive of his daughter.

To Sow Or Not To Sow?

I took an interest in natural principles some years ago. It came by reading the Scriptures. I noticed a great deal of reference made to nature and natural principles. For example, King Solomon, in the book of Proverbs said, "A lazy person should observe the ant, watch her ways, and learn wisdom from it."[2] Anyone who has watched ants know they are the most industrious creatures ever.

Furthermore, anyone who reads or studies the Scriptures knows that many principles are cited using nature - plant and animal life. **My point is that understanding the principles of nature can lead us to a fuller understanding of spiritual reality. Natural principles are a prelude to spiritual principles and truth.**

Likewise, the more parents and people take time to study natural principles, the better the understanding and insight we receive for child-rearing, character development, and relationships.

I have inculcated the wisdom of sowing and reaping in my child-rearing practices with my daughters. I've discovered how to reap rewarding results from parenting. *It all begins with the realization that parenting is sowing.*

After marriage, parenting is the greatest responsibility ever committed to humans. Parenting affects progeny. Progeny affects humanity. As parents, we need all the help we can get. What parents sow or fail to sow within each

[2] Proverbs 6:6-8

female either strengthens or stunts the growth and development of her spirit, soul and body. That's why understanding natural principles is so important in our child-rearing practices. We reap what we sow!

The issue isn't really, "to sow or not to sow." Sowing is inevitable. The real issue is, how and what to sow? I am discovering that numerous parents don't know what seeds to sow or how to sow them.

Let's look at planting a flower garden. The type of flower you want is predicated upon the type of seed you sow. Only a certain seed can produce a certain flower. That's simple enough. But knowing what type of flower you want is not so simple. One must consider environment, climate and soil.

The same natural principles operate in the sowing of a child's character. Parents need to provide the right climate of a loving home, the right seeds, which are natural and spiritual principles, and the correct methods of cultivation. Do these "right" things guarantee children will never go wrong? Certainly not. Our children have the power of choice. But using the right principles give them the advantages they need to properly develop.

A child's character is like a flower garden. Seeds must be planted if character is to develop. Most parents usually sow similar seeds that were sown in them in their childhood and youth. Some seeds inhibited their growth and development. Some seeds enhanced their growth and development. But as the saying goes, "Fruit don't fall too far from the tree." Most people parent like their parents, unless they choose to parent differently.

When a parent doesn't know what type of seeds to sow, that is a problem in itself. Another fact about a character garden is that a parent doesn't have to sow before something can grow. All a parent has to do is leave the garden alone and *something* will eventually spring up! The child may display attitudes, temperament or types of behavior that the parent must spend much of his or her time uprooting *weeds* when he or she should be watering carefully selected and sown seeds of character. We have all seen gardens that have been left unattended. What an unsightly patch of earth!

Sadly, we witness some children and youth who have been neglected and left to grow on their own. To observe their inappropriate behavior or listen to their foul mouths is painful to behold! I'm not blaming nor excusing the victim. We can't condemn the plant. The plant is either productive or problematic. It is a sowing phase that parents must understand.

It is the nature of the seeds, that is, the character, type, sort, kind, essence, basis, constitution, disposition or quality of the seeds, sown in a female, in her upbringing, that determines the yield - her scent and spirit - especially during her defining moments.

Every living thing begins with a seed. Seeds are amazing in themselves. Their nature is as mysterious as their growth. It is mind-boggling to comprehend how seeds grow mainly because their essence is imperceptible to the naked eye. It is their results that become visible to the observer.

The sowing process may be as different as each female, but the principle is the same. Either she is properly seeded or she will be impeded. It is the parents' privilege to empower themselves with the knowledge of seeds and growth.

Not too many parents understand this process. We've been in the city too long! We were created from the soil of the earth, not from asphalt and steel. Asphalt and steel are not receptive to seed. That's why our Creator put our first parents in a garden and not a city. The further we move away from natural principles, the further we move away from proper growth and development. Parenting is sowing.

Females are receivers of seed. With it, they produce seed. This principle of nature is highly disregarded as it relates to the character development of girls-to-women. Much attention is given to the implantation of a male's seed and not enough attention to the kind of seed received by a female.

It is by the study and internalization of our Creator's principles of nature and spiritual principles, that parents gain adequate knowledge and information of the kind of seeds that are essential to sow in our girls. It is by teaching our Creator's natural and spiritual principles to our girls that they learn how to rightly cultivate these good seeds in womanhood.

Seeds Parents Need To Sow

Our Creator has designed nature to offer balance; sunshine and rain, day and night, hot and cold. Each does its part in helping the seed grow rightly. The seed of **balance** must be sown by parents in their daughters. It is balance that most people never attain in life. Obsession, cynicism, and close-mindedness, are some of the fruit of the absence of balance. These weeds must be pruned if one is to attain balance.

When the seed of balance is sown in a girl, she is given the ability to adjust to various encounters in life, without compromising principle, making them work to her benefit. She learns how to roll with the punches so that she is able to stay on her noble course.

A female who is sown and cultivates balance learns how to pick and choose her battles. Like the Scripture says, she doesn't "cast her pearls before swine." Pigs don't appreciate pearls. They only trample them in the mud. She doesn't expend time or energy on issues or people who are unprincipled and self-serving. Societal opposition is too great against females for them not to possess balance.

Balance is necessary for mental and emotional steadiness. Just as balance in nature roots in our Creator's natural principles, balance also has its roots in our Creator's spiritual principles. Balance follows a spiritual and principled path in all challenges and circumstances.

Balance may play a great part in a female choosing her friends. A balanced female may also discern a balanced male or detect whether he is obsessed, controlling, or close-minded. Balance may help females differentiate who will be friends, who will be associates, and who will have to be without their company.

When parents sow and cultivate the seed of balance in their daughters, they may rest easier at night, knowing they have sown in them the ability to discern, deliberate, detect and differentiate wisely.

The **security** of our females is essential. By security, I mean her bread, water and shelter are intact. A girl should not have to worry whether she will have something to eat, drink or a place to live. Parents who take care of these most basic needs help to make their daughters secure.

While security is essential, a girl's **stability** is quintessential. Stability is like the roots of a flower that anchor a female in life's calm and turbulent experiences. If a female is to effectively make her own way in life, stability is necessary. The dictionary defines stability as, "the quality, state or degree of being stable; the strength to stand or endure; firmness."

I like this definition of stability the best: "The property of the body that causes it when disturbed from a condition of equilibrium or steady motion to develop forces or moments that restore the original condition." *A woman's defining moments in life will ultimately reveal her stability or instability.*

Instability is the nemesis of many women. If the veil could be pulled back, it is astounding to find many women, who are put on a pedestal, yet they are unstable in their thoughts, emotions and will. They are masters of disguise! Many women function proficiently on their jobs, but get real shaky when it's time to make important personal and relational decisions. But they should not be blamed. Many of these women have found ways to compensate for not having seeds sown in their childhood that produce stability.

Seeds of a **healthy esteem** and **principled**, **independent thinking** need to be sown in every girl. Without these seeds of character that rightly develop a girl into a woman, her personal worth and individuality are stifled. The absence of a healthy esteem and principled, independent thinking are like petals missing from a flower.

The whole notion of the modern-day independent woman may be more of a cliche' than a reality. Beneath the charming exterior of many independent-type women may just be some inhibiting fears, insecurities, or lack of confidence, although it may not be evident to the natural eye.

On the other hand, there have been, and still are, parents who invest particular time and attention to the sowing process of their daughters. They know the importance of their daughters developing a healthy esteem and becoming a principled, independent thinker.

For clarification purposes, the reason I term it healthy esteem and not self-esteem is that esteem is not self-generated; it is sown or implanted. A child internalizes her or his esteem, or the lack of it, as a response to how she or he is loved, accepted and valued by parents, guardians or their primary care-giver.

Esteem is to be sown and cultivated. A parent can never leave esteem unattended. If so, esteem may wither like an unwatered flower. Esteem must be attended to daily in one way or another. Esteem will not fully blossom if left unattended. Daily affirmations, expressions of love, words of encouragement and appreciation, and the like are the tools that should be used to cultivate a healthy esteem in our females.

The absence of love, acceptance and value results in the absence of esteem. If esteem is not sown, it cannot be cultivated. But something always grows up in the garden where esteem is not planted. The weeds of inferiority complex, dependency, self-hatred, or an obsession for attention, may quickly crop up and take its toll on the child. That's why I believe parents play a most crucial role in sowing and keeping the esteem of their children healthy and growing.

Esteem is the belief one receives and accepts about oneself. Esteem can be cultivated or crushed; kept healthy or become unhealthy. Sowing a healthy esteem in a girl has to start from day one. It begins with words, looks - and get this! - a parent's body language! Our girls should not only hear how they are loved, appreciated and valued; they also have to see it in their parent's eyes and body language.

A parent's eyes and body language are as powerful as the words they speak to their child. A child learns a lot from what they see in their parent's eyes and body language. As, "Smiling Faces," a '70's song says, "The truth is in the eyes and the eyes don't lie, amen!"

A girl must continuously hear and see in her parent's eyes, how loved, appreciated, and valuable she is. Daily, as I drop my two daughters off at school, I tell them, "I love you, I trust you, and I believe in you," before they get out of the car. I say this because I mean it, and because it contributes to them having a healthy esteem.

It is important that my daughters know, hear and see that they are loved, accepted, and valued by their mother and me. And even when they make mistakes, we make sure they know that they are loved and accepted while they make mistakes. It is love and acceptance that helps them grow out of their mistakes.

Knowing they are highly regarded and valued by my wife and me frees our daughters from seeking acceptance based on their performance. When girls are pushed to perform in order to be accepted, this is tantamount to asking them to prostitute themselves. My daughters' esteem is not predicated on what they do, but on who they are. In turn, they have learned to love, appreciate and value themselves. Their principled behavior - what they do - is just the by-product of who they are and to whom they belong. No female should leave home without a healthy esteem.

In developing a **principled, independent thinker**, parents must permit their daughter to verbalize their thoughts and feelings, even when it counters the parents' position or point of view. They must be permitted to disagree with their parents and not worry about negative repercussion or retaliation. Having said that, females have to be taught there is an appropriate time and a respectful way that they should verbalize their thoughts and feelings.

Some females are trained to subordinate their independent thinking, parrot parents, or acquiesce to popular public sentiment. In the words of one author, they are trained to be, "mere reflectors of other men's thoughts."

Some females are instructed that their best position is to be all things to all people and offend none. This is supposed to lessen their opposition and increase their opportunities, personal and professional. Hogwash! Every female needs to know that principled, independent thinkers must take a stand! Even if an opportunity is denied her because of her stand for truth or principle, she still retains her integrity.

Unfortunately, to be a principled, independent thinker in our society is viewed as the exception, not the rule. Many females have painful regrets because they have been trained or have chosen to compromise just to be recognized. But when the seeds of a healthy esteem and principled, independent thinker are sown and cultivated, although a female may face serious opposition at times, she can remain unbought and unashamed.

Other seeds sown in the garden of character that help our females blossom and reach their fullest potential are **trust** and the necessity of cultivating **personal responsibility.**

Trust is one of the most powerful virtues of character that can be bestowed on a female in her upbringing. Trust gives children freedom to grow, but within certain boundaries. I say this from personal experience. My mother trusted me. Her trust was as important to me as her love. I didn't want to violate her trust in me. There were things I would not do because she trusted me. Her trust defined my boundaries.

Trust is like a fence at the top of a high cliff. As long as a child operates within its boundaries, they are free. Going outside the boundaries of trust will bring pain and regret.

The seed of trust must be cultivated wisely by parents if it is to do all it's intended to do. Trust should not be handled like a whip for achieving behavior modification. That's taking trust out of its proper context and using it to manipulate our females' behavior instead of empowering them for personal responsibility.

Also, trust is not like a wage that a child must earn like a paycheck. Trust is a priceless gift that a parent should give freely. A female's growth is stunted if she feels she has to earn her parent's trust. I know that some of you reading the previous sentence may have a point of departure with me. It's okay to disagree with me, but hear me out.

My point of reference is my own upbringing. I didn't have to prove myself worthy before I earned my parent's trust. Neither do my daughters have to earn my trust. My wife and I gladly give it to them. It is their birthright. It comes with the package deal, the signing bonus, with being born into our family! In my home, trust is to be maintained, not earned.

Because females are the receiver of seed and the bearer of seed, most females are vicariously made 'suspect,' especially as it has to do with their sexuality. A lot more demands, threats, and innuendo are directed toward them. Caution and concern are always in order, but a female should not be mistrusted because she has been endowed with the ability to procreate. It is also wrong to equate a female's singleness with promiscuity.

It's how a parent handles trust that makes it a blessing or a curse. When my two daughters' menstruation period had come, my wife and I *celebrated* this gift of nature by our family going out to dinner! We wanted them to understand that having the ability to receive seed and procreate is a special, sacred gift from our Creator. It's a time to celebrate!

We use no threats or scare tactics to coerce them to maintain their virginity until marriage. We use adequate and complete information. We use love, appreciation, value and trust. If that can't do the job, nothing else will.

We wanted them to know that they had come to a special time in their lives of trust and responsibility. *Trust should be used as a milestone, not a millstone!* My wife and I are committed to instill in our daughters a healthy concept of themselves and their sexuality.

Trust should be like the sun that hovers over a flower. It bathes and encircles in its warmth. Few virtues, if any, are more reassuring to the stability, growth and development of a female than to be trusted.

As I previously stated, my mother trusted me. She didn't expect me to violate her trust, but knowing I was human, she told me if I ever did, she would still love me and her trust in me could be restored. I've never lied to her. I never wanted to violate her trust in me.

That's why I know that the seed of trust must be sown in girls. Sooner or later, parents are going to have to let them go out at night. Like those seeds that may travel short or long distances, sooner or later, females have to make their own way in life. They need to be empowered to fly high toward their calling in life! Without trust, they may become tumbleweeds, unstable and blowing about without direction or destination.

How many females and males do we know who are now tumbleweeds because their father or mother were tumbleweeds? How many females have had some of their dreams deferred or their aspirations temporarily impeded before they have gotten out of their teens? How many males, like tumble weeds, are spreading their seeds all over town?

With trust comes **personal responsibility**. One of the greatest comforts to a parent is to know they can give their daughter or son a responsibility and know that it will be done right the first time and in a timely manner. I told my daughters that their work is their signature. They are signing their name and their family name to their work. Their work should be of such quality work that there is no question who did it!

Starting and completing chores around the house helps to stabilize them in personal responsibility. Completing assignments, involving them in community service work, and becoming gainfully employed as a teenager, all support the cultivation of personal responsibility in them.

Accepting personal responsibility affects their choices and decisions. Our Creator has equipped us with the freedom of choice. After the gift of love, I believe that the second greatest gift from our Creator is choice. Choice and personal responsibility are inseparably linked. Each child will experience the rewards or regrets of this freedom of choice. *Personal responsibility is to manage choice.*

It is not certain where each woman will finally land, but if parents have seeded their daughter with trust and personal responsibility, they may travel far and wide, or they may simply be at a friend's house across town, but there is a peace a trusting parent can experience.

The appreciation and affirmation of **cultural identity** is of utmost importance if a female is to be seeded in her own cultural soil and stay connected to her roots. Any flower that is uprooted withers and dies.

The respect and appreciation for one's own cultural identity should be sown in such a way that gives every female a respect for all humanity. They must know that each culture is like a distinct and unique flower in a bouquet. The bouquet only exists because they are part and parcel of it.

Our Creator is not color blind. Color-blindness does not make an ideal society. Colors do matter. Variety is said to be the spice of life. Cultural identity matters. It connects a female to a point of reference; it roots and grounds her. Thus, she is able to share in the trials and triumphs of her people's past, the possibilities of their present, and faith for their future.

As it pertains to assisting our females in developing a healthy cultural identity, I believe the late African ancestor, Sun Ra said it best, "If you are not your own reality, then whose myth are you?" A female without a healthy cultural identity may lack essential nourishment from her cultural community.

It is impossible for me to share all the essential seeds of character that help girls bloom into womanhood. I am only sharing some of the seeds my wife and I deem necessary for our daughters to grow up healthy and productive.

The last, but certainly not the least of attributes that must be sown in each girl is **vision.** The Scripture says, "Where there is no vision, the people perish."[3]

Although each female takes a different path, there is still a divine objective, a higher calling for each of them that is to be discovered and accomplished. Our Creator has no useless seeds. They all have a specific time and purpose.

All females need to know that they have been granted the gift of life for a special purpose. Daily, we witness females who have yet to realize this fact and wander aimlessly without vision.

A female who possesses a noble vision is like a flower moving steadily toward full fruition. Her progress may be gradual, but it is constant. Even in her setbacks, her vision is not dimmed. She becomes more determined.

But a female can't be what she can't see. That's why the seed of vision has to be planted in her mind as a necessary part of her sowing. Our daughters must be reminded that all life has purpose, thus, they have a divine purpose to fulfill. Parents can't give vision. Only our Creator's Spirit does that. But parents can best position their daughters to receive it.

[3] Proverbs 29:18

Just as a gardener positions a flower where it can best fulfill its purpose, so parents must put their daughters in the best position to understand and receive vision. That position is almost always *not* in front of a television. T.V. watching is a passive activity. Nothing is left to the imagination.

Sowing vision in females comes partly through giving them a love for reading wholesome and inspiring books, providing them with mentors at different stages of their growth and development, and giving them access to people, presentations, conferences, retreats and opportunities that provide them with truthful information, instruction, and inspiration. These are some of the many things parents can do to properly position their daughters for vision.

One of life's greatest attainments is to become what one has been created to be. Without a vision or mission in life, a female may become very successful by society's standards, but very unfulfilled in her life and spirit. Visions are for the purpose of helping, healing, directing, and empowering people. True visionaries are other-people-minded.

Once our females have a vision, it is the parents and the villages' responsibility to make provision for them to fulfill their vision. We must bring to bear whatever human and material resources that is needed to help them fulfill their vision. No child or youth should be without a support system for her or his vision.

In summation, it is the sacred privilege of parenting to identify and sow specific seeds in our females that will bear fruit to the health and well-being of their spirit, soul, body, as well as their male-female relationships.

Balance, security, stability, a healthy esteem, principled-independent thinking, trust, personal responsibility, cultural identity and vision, are necessary seeds for a girl and makes pruning as a woman, minimal.

As I quoted in my book, *Smellin' Ourselves*, "It is easier to build a boy than it is to mend a man." The same principle applies to our girls. **It is easier to sow good seeds in a girl than it is to prune a woman.**

I have sought to share some insight into the benefit and blessing of understanding and inculcating natural principles in child-rearing practices. Knowing the potential of each seed to take root and eventually produce its own fruit should command the attention and accountability of every parent. If for no other reason, it's because each seed bears after its own kind. That is a natural and spiritual law.

A seed cannot grow until pollen is transferred from the stamen to the pistil. This transfer is called pollination. Since flowers cannot go after pollen, they depend upon some carrier to bring it to them. Flowers are pollinated by flies, moths, wasps, bees, and sometimes hummingbirds.

By their fragrance and color they advertise their sweets - the nectar in the heart of the flower. This is the reward the flower offers its helpers. To reach the nectar, insects must crawl over the pistils and anthers into the heart of the flower. Their bodies become covered with pollen dust. As they move from flower to flower, they transfer the pollen of one to the stigma of another.

Pollen lodges on the stigma of a flower. The pollen tube grows down through the pistil and into the ovary and the egg cell, or ovule, inside the ovary. When the contents of the pollen tube enter the ovule, the flower is fertilized. Important changes begin to take place. The wall of the ovule hardens and becomes a protective coat called the testa. Inside the testa is the embryo, or young plant. Unless conditions are right, seeds will not germinate. However, they may remain alive, or viable, for some time.[1]

[1] Microsoft Encarta 97 Encyclopedia

Pollinating

If I were asked to choose one word that is fundamental to all humanity, it would be *relationships*. Nothing in nature exists unto itself; neither can humans. Our Creator made relationships the tie that binds us together.

As was stated in the beginning of this chapter, "Since flowers cannot go after pollen, they depend upon some carrier to bring it to them." Pollinating is a process of transference of that which is essential for growth and development.

Pollinating, which has all to do with relationships, is akin to human reproduction. The seed, ovary, egg and embryo of a plant suggests similarities. A seed cannot grow by itself. It needs to be pollinated. A specific kind of relationship with that plant must take place if it is to finally blossom into a flower. And so it is with a female.

A female needs specific kinds of pollinating relationships - in her home, community, school, church or place of fellowship, even social interaction - if her spirit, which is the essential or activating principle of her whole being is to develop and mature and bring forth an enhancing scent.

Just as flowers are dependent upon carriers to pollinate the heart of the flower, young girls need carriers of right examples, right information, right instruction and right guidance. Parents are to surround their daughters with certain kinds of adults who know they are "carriers," and know what, when and how to disseminate it to their daughters.

My wife and I have sought to do this very thing. We have asked specific persons in the village to assist us in the growth and development of our daughters in specific ways.

For instance, both of our daughters are musically gifted. We've ask accomplished adult musicians to develop their gifts in piano and voice. The village must be part of the pollinating process of females.

Unfortunately, there are good carriers and not-so-good carriers. Persons who come into a close relationship with females are carriers of some type of "pollen." They may be carriers of negative pollen. That's why parents have to monitor their daughter's male and female associations. We have to help them discern positive carriers from the not-so-positive carriers.

Because of a female's ability to reproduce, pollen enters the very core of her being - her spirit - and gives birth to her words, thoughts, deeds and actions. There are no experiences or encounters that do not affect a female's spirit. Pollinating can even start with a child in the womb!

There was a mother who brought her adopted four year-old girl to our office for intervention. This girl's anger was frightening! Whatever this girl experienced from her biological mother, while this girl was in her womb, was so traumatic, that this young girl was lashing out, hitting and scratching anyone in arms-reach! And this angry little girl had no idea what was going on in her spirit, soul or body!

Pollinating is essentially the act of transference. A child will receive the blessing or the brunt of a parent's predominant spirit. The brunt of a parent's anger, insecurity, apathy or fear, are inevitably pollinating the spirit of the child. Likewise, a parent's spirit of optimism, kindness, confidence or patience, are blessings that benefit their children.

Pollinating is caught and taught. Females are to learn from observation and instruction. That's how my mother pollinated her four children. She just didn't tell us to scrub the floor; she showed us how to scrub it. She got on her hands and knees (we never owned a mop - my mother said you can't get in the corners with a mop!) and through observation and instruction, we learned how to scrub a floor and do it right the first time!

In short, parents are carriers. We usually transfer to our children *what* and *how* it was transferred to us. Note that I said, "usually." Some of your pollinating experiences were so painful that you refuse to replicate your parent's spirit and methods. Nevertheless, you must remain vigilant or you may find yourself reverting to similar methods.

Pollination precedes germination. Germination, the act of sprouting or coming into being, is essential to the growth and development of the flower. The conditions must be right if a seed is to germinate. Germination is the natural result of a seed that has been rightly pollinated. If a seed does not germinate, growth and development are inhibited.

The more I understand pollination and germination - one is cause; the other, effect - I realized that as a father of two daughters, I play a primary role in hindering or helping my daughters develop a healthy attitude about themselves first, and then males.

This book is not a book on horticulture. Rather, it is about male-female relationships. I am simply using the natural principles of the sowing, pollinating and germinating process of flowers to show how the growth and development of females may be inhibited or enhanced in their male-female relationships. Once we know the root, we can understand the fruit.

I have chosen to give my daughters' growth and development my full and complete attention. I can't afford to slack off, get too busy, be inconsistent, or allow any weeds to grow in their character. I must be vigilant on my watch to observe all their male and female associations with whom they are interacting. When or should my daughters say, "I do," I plan to be able to stand tall and with honor and joy, and present them to a husband whose character has been properly developed as well.

If fathers would only recognize, as I have come to understand, that much of the future of their daughter's male-female relationships hinges on the kind of man and father we have been to our daughters, there might be less absentee fathers!

The immutable principle of nature is that all seed-bearing life produces after its own kind. Understanding the unchangeable law of return, if parents are to reap balanced, principled women, and possibly, future mothers, parents will be extremely attentive, patient, principled and consistent in their sowing and pollinating practices.

I have tried to share with you my foundational concept on the proper growth and development of a female by using the comparative analysis of the growth and development of a flower. I encourage you to reread it, process the concept and inculcate it into your child-rearing practices. Understanding natural principles are a prelude to understanding spiritual reality.

Unfortunately, many females have experienced what a botanist refers to as, "growths or formations" that are injurious to the plant. These growths and formations threaten the very existence of the plant and must be *pruned.*

I have come up with my own proverb that applies to women: **"It is easier to sow good seeds and pollinate a girl than it is to prune a woman."**

The Absent Father Complex

To be honest, I didn't know where to put this chapter, but I knew it had to be in here somewhere. My original plan was to have concurrent chapters, Sowing, Pollinating and Pruning. It just seemed to me like a natural flow.

But maybe by inserting this chapter right here, it might just disturb the natural flow of this book. But in some way or another, that is precisely what has happened to more women than can be counted! Their natural growth and development from girlhood to womanhood has been disturbed in some way or another by a man called, *father.*

The absent father complex seems not to be the exception, but the rule! Millions of women's fathers have been absent or not a part of their daughter's growth and development.

This is no small issue. Many women know deep in their spirit that because they had an absent father, they live with a void that only their father, and no other man, could fill. That does not make them any less capable of attaining success in life or wholesome male-female relationships. But more often than not, the absent father complex does impact on a female's relationships with men.

What I'm about to say is not the "law and the gospel," but I have found it to be fairly accurate in my counseling and observations of women who have experienced the absent father complex. *Females who have had a good father that was present and/or available in their childhood and youth seem to be less inhibited and more settled as individuals.* When a female's father is her point of reference as to what constitutes balanced and sensitive manhood, she does not need a man in her life to make her feel complete. She is usually self-confident and secure within herself. She doesn't settle for any man. Her father has given her a model of manhood and she generally looks for a man who holds her father's principles and particulars.

Let me just add that this type of secure female is not the "I don't need a man!" type of female. She respects and enjoys men. She maintains a healthy attitude about men, even when she has experienced not-so-positive men. But she knows the kind of man that was modeled, which is the kind of man she wants, and she is willing to wait, even if it takes a while longer to find him or for him to find her.

Conversely, I have counseled and observed females who have experienced the absent father complex and many (not all) of them are either promiscuous or have difficulty accepting genuine love from a good man. There is a marked difference in the way women (whose fathers were present and available) relate to men, and women whose fathers were not. There is no substitute for the love, appreciation and respect for manhood that a father instills in his daughter. It makes a difference in her personal and professional relationships with men.

I'm simply suggesting from my counseling and observations that a female who does not have a father (or a principled grandfather, uncle, or man in her upbringing) usually has submerged inhibitions that will eventually surface in not-so-positive ways in her relationships with men.

Not enough women are admitting or addressing the fact that they have been inhibited socially by the absent father complex. Although the complex varies among women, the fact remains that although women who have experienced the absent father complex react differently, they have a common denominator: **Their biological father missed his once-in-a-lifetime opportunity to positively involve him-**

self in his daughter's growth and development. His most influential time to be a positive point of reference in his daughter's male concept was lost.

I want to share one out of a myriad of regrettable experiences the affect the absent father complex has on women:

J was a very observant child. Very little escaped her notice. At a very early age, she observed how her father treated her mother. Her parents argued a lot. Sometimes, her father became physical with her mother, though he always came out on the losing end!

As **J** grew older, she couldn't understand why her mother continued to stay in that marital situation. Although her father worked every day, **J** watched as her mother virtually carried the load - children, financial, character development, home upkeep, even college tuition - while her father followed his own self-indulgent agenda.

J's father was in the house but unavailable in terms of being the kind of father to help **J** develop a healthy respect and appreciation for men. Because the conditions were not right, germination never took place. Very early in life, **J**'s concept of men was set in stone: *Remain skeptical of men. Don't let your guard down. Protect yourself. Stay in control.*

J mirrors a host of women whose father was either not present in the home or was present in the home but not available for his daughters. That may be onc of the most disheartening memories that many women have, that is, their father was in the home, but did not give of himself or share the essentials of life his daughter needed. So many fathers failed to impart the example or instructions that give daughters the foundation to love and respect men.

And then there were some fathers in the home who were so completely dominated by their wives, that their daughters did not respect them for being so passive. Their daughters, now women, try to dominate the men in their relationships. That's the image their father gave them about men.

Whether in the home or not, many fathers missed their once-in-a-lifetime opportunity to provide only what a father, and no other man can provide for his daughters. Even though many women have moved on in life, they know there is still a void, like a missing piece in a puzzle, that has not been filled. That void or missing piece is a loving, caring, patient, informative, fun-loving, ever-present, and respected *father*.

This benign neglect usually spells t-r-o-u-b-l-e for a woman's future male-female relationships. Consequently, **J** left home with a vague, distorted, and incomplete view of what a man should be, and how to relate to men. These submerged distortions in her spirit eventually surfaced in **J**'s marriage and family.

J's rigid spirit also had a profound impact on the way in which she reared her children. Years later, especially in her defining moments, as it concerned her daughter and husband, **J** would emit scents that would seriously inhibit her marital and family relationships.

J is like a snapdragon, a closed flower, always in reserve, not fully trusting men, even fearing the worst. With her husband, **J** has yet to fully open up her spirit, soul or body to him. The reality is that **J**'s father never sowed the seed of trust in her, as it concerned men. One reason was that **J**'s father proved untrustworthy by having extramarital encounters. **J**'s father's infidelity impacted her thinking about men, and even cast a cloud of mistrust over **J**'s husband.

To keep from going through what **J**'s mother had endured, or from getting hurt, **J** took on some inflexible positions in her marriage and family. There were things she would not tolerate from her husband, and if it ever happened, she is out the door! No looking back!

When issues came up in her home, **J** would nip them in the bud quick! The problem with **J** was not what she addressed, but the spirit in which she addressed them. If her children did something wrong, they felt the brunt of her wrath! Her displeasure was not only in her voice, but in her eyes and body language. Her scent become unbearable!

As well-meaning and as interested as **J** was in her children learning right from wrong, her children had a difficult time seeing her good intentions in correcting them, because her methods were so glaringly punitive. Mercy seemed few and far between!

Let me say for the record that **J** is not a monster. **J** has a great sense of humor. She's personable and - boy! - does she have skills! She's quick thinking, a conceptual learner, razor sharp intuition, and can cook out of this world! **J** is very committed to her children's success, and actively involved with the children and youth in her church.

At the same time, **J**'s spirit has made it difficult for her own children to grow and blossom in their spirit. She is doing to her children's spirit what her father did to hers, filling it with a resentment that is submerged deep in their spirit, so deep it is imperceptible to the naked eye, but it's there.

J's daughter has suffered the most from **J**'s punitive and controlling spirit. **J** will have to recognize that she is responsible for the lion's share of her daughter's interrupted spirit. **J** helped interrupt it, and **J** can help free it! The transference of **J**'s spirit to her daughter was so subtle that **J**, observant as she is, hasn't discerned the magnitude of it. **J** has weighted, wounded and oppressed her daughter's spirit. Her daughter is having one difficulty after another.

Until **J** admits and seeks intervention for her own interrupted spirit, it will be difficult for her to help recover and restore her daughter's spirit to a state of normalcy. Ironically, her daughter is looked on by **J** as the one who has the problem, but **J** does not see herself as part of it.

J is almost always right, as far as she is concerned. It's either right or wrong. Seldom does she try to find middle ground. **J** is obsessed with control, not control from a power point of view, but she is afraid not to be in control of every situation in her marriage, family and home.

This obsession for control continues to affect her relationship with her children. She seldom gives them the longitude or latitude to think for themselves. She is always telling them what to do, what not to do, and how it should or should not be done. If they disagree or have a different view, **J** sees them as uncooperative, disobedient or rebellious, depending upon what **J** thinks they ought to do and how she wants them to do it.

For **J**, control is her ultimate form of self-protection. She controls because she has not admitted, much less, evicted the skeletons of her father out of her spirit. To relinquish control over every situation would make her vulnerable to be hurt, mistreated or repeat her mother's experience, and that won't happen in a million years, if she has her way!

So **J** regulates her children to the point that they despise her methods, and probably her, sometimes, if one could get them to admit it. I'll just call it a love-hate relationship. They love her and hate her controlling, punitive methods and spirit. It's the same love-hate thing **J** has for her father.

The most unfortunate thing about this is that **J**'s children won't confront her about it. Until they address it, they may function, and do well in life, but not healed in their spirit, as it pertains to their mother. But J won't confront her father either, so her spirit has yet to be recovered or restored to a state of normalcy. Both **J** and her children probably figure it won't do any good, so they just leave it alone.

J's father has never made an attempt to rectify, much less, admit his flagrant wrongs or shortcomings with **J**'s mother or **J**. Nor has **J** made a full and complete attempt to mend fences with her own children. So **J**'s spirit remains interrupted, and so does her children's.

J's husband loves **J**. He is one of the most loving, sharing, spiritual men one will ever meet. **J** knows he is a good man, but she does not see him as he is. She sees him through the lens of her father. This is not fair to **J**'s husband.

Because **J** has held herself in reserve, she has not given her husband what he needs to feel stable and secure in his marriage with her. **J** has a very keen capacity to discern people and situations. Should her husband approach people or situations his way his spirit is led, instead of heeding **J**'s counsel, **J** doesn't take it too well. **J** has to try and control him if she is to keep him from becoming what her father was to her mother. Skeletons!

J has a tendency to be more critical than affirming. Her husband needs a lot of affirmation. He is also the huggy-touchy type, but **J** doesn't like him to be romantic with her in public, nor does she initiate it publically. When he tries to display affection in public, **J** resists his advances.

Like a snapdragon flower, **J** closed up her spirit early in life, all because of her observation and inattention of her father. I don't think **J** recognizes her unpleasant scents as a mother and wife - controlling, inflexible and punitive.

With all the gifts, talents, and abilities **J** has been blessed with, **J** has yet to open up and reach her fullest potential. **J**'s father could do a lot to remedy her situation, but it seems unlikely that he will, unless it's a death-bed confession! So many fathers have gone to their grave without admitting or seeking to "make it right" with their wives and children.

Even if this was not your exact experience, many women identify with **J**. Although you function well in public, in your home or male relationships, you have to be in control. It's a defense mechanism because you saw what your mother went through with your father and you can't let that happen to you! **J** and many women are like a Snapdragon flower. It's hard to open up and acknowledge your scent.

Opening A Snapdragon's Spirit

In my research of the snapdragon, the lower lip of the large tubular petal snaps shut if opened. The lip-like petals provide a place where a bee can land before entering. When a bumblebee alights on the lip of a snapdragon, the bumblebee's weight, which is greater than that of most bees, opens the flower's mouth, letting the bee enter the inner chamber to pollinate it and sip the nectar.[1]

The recovery and restoration of J's spirit to a state of normalcy pivots on whether she will permit herself to be opened. A snapdragon's spirit cannot be restored unless opened, so that she can rid herself of her "foul scents" that has inhibited her marital and family relationships.

Snapdragons have to: 1) open up and express how they really feel about their father; 2) be open to principled intervention; 3) be open to change, especially in the areas where they have been resistant or snap shut when confronted; 4) and open to confessing and forsaking their wrong spirit and methods so they can be healed.

1. Open up and express how you really feel about your father. Although snapdragons like **J** have come forth from this type of situation and excelled in career-life, they know there is a void, a missing portion, however large or small, in their spirit that no one but their father can fill. Many of

[1] Microsoft Encarta 97 Encyclopedia

these women have yet to move beyond their father's long, haunting shadow.

I've counseled or dialogued with women whose fathers were neither present nor available for them. It has deeply inhibited their spirit, their thoughts, emotions and will, and sometimes, their physical health.

If the father is alive, **J** and other snapdragons will have to take the initiative to have a heart-to-heart talk with him, if at all possible. This is purging the soul of the thoughts and emotions that have impeded her life and relationships.

If talking face to face is impossible because he is deceased or incapacitated in his cognitive abilities, his refusal to talk, or some other reason, *write a letter*. Now you have the time to say all you need to say, and say it! Let it out! My suggestion is that you write what I call a "sandwich."

First, *affirm*. If there is anything positive that you can say about your father, or an expression of appreciation to him, let your letter begin with it. Affirmation opens the spirit. If you start by attacking him, he will close up. You plant a seed by opening the ground, not closing it.

Secondly, *say all you need to say*. This is the "garden burger" between the bread. This is the reason for the sandwich. Saying all you need to say may take 40 pages. So be it. Get it out, get it out, get it out! Just do it in a respectful way. Take the high road.

Finally, *give suggestions*. Share with your father how you think issues between you and him can be resolved. For women whose fathers are deceased, since you can't make suggestions, make the final part of your letter what you have resolved to do from that point on with your life. But still write that letter! It will help bring closure. You need it.

Your father may or may not admit and apologize for the error of his ways. If he does, fine. If not, what you have done is purge your soul of the things you have been thinking and feeling about him all these years. This is also your time to open your spirit and release the scents that inhibit your male-female relationships and family harmony.

2. Be open to principled intervention. Principled intervention is necessary to work the inhibiting scents out of one's spirit. It may come through counseling, a support group, or reading self-help material. But whatever the venue, it must be spiritual, principled and based on truth.

Snapdragons are used to handling things themselves. It is a challenge for them to open themselves up to another perspective. But if you desire a restoration of your spirit to a state of normalcy, you need some form of intervention.

3. Be open to change, especially in the areas where you have been resistant or snap shut when confronted. J's predominant inhibiting scents are from a spirit that is controlling, inflexible and punitive. She may disagree or try to justify why she reacts that way. A snapdragon will have to differentiate those who criticize from those who want the best for them.

J is going to have to listen and accept the words of those she loves and who love her. She has to be open enough to ask her children and her husband about her spirit toward them. **J** has a spiritual, balanced mother who she can listen to and accept her counsel. **J** has brothers who know her and will wholeheartedly support her recovery and restoration of spirit back to a state of normalcy.

It is in the context of loving relationships that **J** can drop her resistant spirit and open herself for healing. With the absence of condemnation and blame, **J** and other snapdragons may come forth. This does not excuse snapdragons from being accountable for their actions. Snapdragons are highly sensitive and quite emotional so the right people must be available and supportive for them to open up fully.

4. Be open to confessing and forsaking your wrong spirit and methods so you can be healed. The damage has been done. You are not responsible for the spirit that was or was not developed in you. You were the recipient, not the initiator. But you are accountable for rectifying your wrong spirit and methods toward your husband, man, and/or children. Confess it to them. Ask for their forgiveness.

This is purging. It is also letting them know that they don't have to be victims anymore. They are free, if they choose, to forgive you. If they refuse your sincere confession and request for forgiveness, they bind themselves from then on until they forgive. Forgive yourself and go on.

Summation

As aforementioned, I have counseled many women who still experience a void in their lives because their fathers were not present or unavailable to them. This has certainly affected their view of men and impeded in some way their male-female relationships. Yet, what your father has done or not done in the past, cannot keep you from living a fulfilled life. That's your decision.

But let me caution you. If you are not open to those four steps of recovery and restoration of spirit, then like a heavy bumblebee that forces open the petal of the snapdragon to get inside, it might take a profound or tragic experience in your life, marriage or family, to force open your spirit, so that help, hope and healing may begin.

But no matter what past experiences a snapdragon has encountered, our Creator's Spirit is ever-present and available to lead and guide you into a blessed and productive future. My favorite quote is, "Where there is life, there is hope."

Pruning is the removal of parts of woody plants, usually branches or branch tips, to relieve the burden on the remaining parts of the plant, to cut out diseased or broken parts, to increase the quantity and quality of flowers or fruits, to train individual parts to positions structurally favorable to the health of the plant, or to shape the plant into another form.

When the branches of trees and/or shrubs are pruned, wood or stem production is encouraged; the pruning of roots reduces wood production but increases fruit bearing.[1]

[1] Compton's Interactive Encyclopedia

Pruning

Daily, the spirit, soul and body of girls are interrupted, usually by someone they know well. These interruptions cause them considerable discomfort or pain. When a woman's spirit is weighted, wounded, oppressed or violated, she cannot function in a state of normalcy.

The libraries of the world cannot contain the volumes that can be written about girls who have been made to suffer in spirit, soul and body. And not only by males, but also by females - mothers, stepmothers, grandmothers, aunts, sisters, cousins, and so-called, girl friends.

These inexcusable experiences and encounters inevitably cause growths and formations on a female's spirit. Lingering bitterness, anger, hurt, hatred, and for an increasing number of women, depression, interrupt the spirit of girls and women and inhibit the proper functioning of their soul and body.

These, and other inhibiting growths and formations must be pruned out of a woman's spirit. Only then can her soul - thoughts, emotions and will, and physical health have the best chance of restoration.

In plant life, pruning is essential in bringing forth a new, strong plant or flower. One of the reasons many women are prisoners of their past, present, and future in male-female relationships is, they have not been pruned in their spirit. Many women have brought unresolved issues from their childhood and youth into their male-female relationships, marriages and family. Some women's scent can be so obnoxious at times that their own family seeks to steer clear of them!

Pruning hurts. I can imagine if the flowers or plants

could talk, they would probably articulate the searing pain of the serpette, the sharp pruning knife. As humans, we know that any incision in our flesh, with the absence of anesthesia, is painful. The incision of the pruning knife in a woman's spirit, the most sensitive area of her whole being, has to be very painful.

The emotions of the soul are the medium through which the spirit's pain is expressed. I view emotions, not only as a true indicator of our spirit, but also as a release valve for our spirit. Emotions tell us whether what's going on in our spirit is right or wrong, healthy or unhealthy.

Most women have no problem showing or expressing their emotions. That's why I believe women, in general, are better positioned to receive healing and restoration far more than men. Most men won't let their true emotions out. This in turn, stifles men from opening their spirit to be recovered and restored from the weights, wounds, oppression or violation men have received from their upbringing, interpersonal encounters, and/or from a women.

As I researched the pruning process, it became evident to me that pruning is virtually a life or death issue! Please don't miss that. The longevity, even the very life of an affected or infected plant is dependent upon it being pruned.

The purpose of pruning is: 1) the removal of certain parts of a plant to relieve the burden on the remaining parts of the plant; 2) cutting out diseased or broken parts and increase the quantity and quality of flowers or fruits; 3) train individual parts to positions structurally favorable to the health of the plant; 4) shape the plant.[2]

The removal of certain parts of a plant to relieve the burden on the remaining parts of the plant. This pruning

[2] Compton's Interactive Encyclopedia

addresses women who are *weighted* in spirit. A woman may not be responsible for her burdens, but she is accountable for unloading them. Relieving herself of burdens is critical to a woman's future and forward progress. The weights on a woman's spirit certainly impedes her mental, emotional and physical health.

Cutting out diseased or broken parts and increase the quantity and quality of flowers or fruits. Most women have never reached their maximal potential because they have been *wounded* in their spirit. If these women are to aspire to their maximal potential and experience fulfillment, they must take the initiative to prune out all that is causing them "dis-ease" in spirit and prohibiting them from bearing fruit.

To train individual parts to positions structurally favorable to the health of the plant. The spirit of many women has been *oppressed*. The oppression of women has all to do with the positioning or subjugation of women by any means necessary. Pruning that which has caused oppression must take place if such women are to reposition themselves in an effort to restore their health and well-being.

To shape the plant. A *violated* spirit can reshape a woman's whole life. Pruning is a way of removing damaged or terminal formations stimulated by an injury that restrict the plant's growth and development. Pruning can stimulate the shape or direction a woman's life will take.

Understanding my comparison of pruning plants and pruning weighted, wounded, oppressed or violated spirits is of utmost importance. It should encourage women that no matter what situation or circumstance they have experienced, encountered, or even succumbed to their detriment, there is a possibility as well as a process of restoration!

And don't overlook the fact that pruning may determine future growth of a woman who is willing to go under the knife. Many plants blossom more abundantly after pruning. Pruned plants often yield bigger and better fruit!

To refuse the pruning knife, even to procrastinate, is detrimental, and in the extreme, fatal, for some women who resist having their inhibiting growths and formations pruned from their spirit. **Pruning is a necessary recourse to survival, sanity and salvation of many women.**

Women who have support and encouragement have a better chance of being recovered and restored in spirit. *Although the pruning process may take longer for some women than others, the pace of the pruning process is the same for all women, one day at a time.* Each day holds the possibility of restoration, but pruning is an individual decision.

In the following chapters, I will share three predominant scents I have observed in many women that inhibit their male-female relationships. Although there are many inhibiting scents of a woman, these three continue to surface more than others in my counseling and contact with women.

Please understand that these scents of a woman only scratch the surface, as it pertains to women in need of pruning. If something I say encourages the recovery and restoration of a woman's spirit, our Creator be praised!

I also want to share three predominant scents of a woman that enhance male-female relationships. I know these scents enhance because my wife continually releases them into the atmosphere of our marriage and family relationship.

Warning: If you go beyond this point, you will be entering the pruning room. "Scalpel, please!"

Inhibiting Scents Of A Woman

Generally, women bear the brunt of most male-female relationships. The centuries of patriarchy, sexism and chauvinism, bring me to that conclusion. These sins not just in dating or marital relationships. They are also in political, economic, social and religious male-female relationships; women of color catching hades the most.

Although the structures of this male-dominated society tips the scales in favor of men, yet, many woman have been, and continue to be at fault in the fracturing of male-female relationships. I vividly remember that I was fired by a woman supervisor unjustly. Some women have even gotten away with unjustifiable murder!

Because the onus of responsibility is usually placed on men in male-female relationships, men are usually scrutinized more thoroughly than women. It is often assumed, until further investigation, that the man is the initiator or violator. This unfortunate posture diverts the spotlight away from women who are the culprit in male-female relationships.

The changes that some women take their men through, is not nearly cited like the voluminous books and articles that chronicle the offenses of men against women! Where are the best sellers by or about men who have been done in by women? Most men probably don't live to write about it anyway!

There are some things that women have done to men in male-female relationships that stagger the imagination and defy reason! I don't think most men can conjure up half of things some women have. A lot of it probably comes out of a woman's pain, desire for retaliation, or plain, old spite.

I mentioned in my book, *Smellin' Ourselves: What Men Need To Understand About Ourselves And Our Women,* how a woman accused her daughter's father of sexually molesting their daughter, and it was a bold face lie! He had to go through the whole court fiasco, and in the court of public opinion, he was dubbed guilty simply by being accused. The woman did it for spite. Not even with his "not guilty" verdict has he been completely exonerated in the minds of some people! The vindictive scent (spirit) of this woman has caused untold suffering for this man and his daughter.

Now, there are times, unbeknownst to some women, when they exude an inhibiting scent into their male-female relationship. These are times when under duress or off-guard, they say or react in a way that is not their normal modus operandi. When that word, look, or reaction is brought to their attention, they immediately and sincerely rectify it. The inhibiting scent they released into the atmosphere of their male-female relationship quickly dissipates.

But some women have long and lingering scents that continue to inhibit their male-female relationships. Some of these scents make it difficult for some men to endure or live with. They get their hats and are out the door! Such is the case for many former husbands, some, who are fathers, who have had to take up another residence apart from their children. Irregardless, a man should always do right by his children. A father should assume financial and moral responsibility for his children. *But men hurt as bad as women hurt.*

Some men have tried their best to stick it out and make the best of their marriage. They've sought principled intervention, but their wives were uncooperative, to say the least. It's not always the man's fault that the marriage or relationship doesn't work. Countless women have lost good men by disregarding their man's spirit.

Women weight, wound, oppress and violate men's spirits on a regular basis. When a man's spirit is weighted, wounded, oppressed or violated, it's difficult for him to function in a state of normalcy. Most men try hard to hide their pain. They don't want to appear weak. But in their spirit, they are hurting, and some men - seriously depressed- over their male-female relationship.

If men were as open as women, and used all the public and private forums that women use to communicate their pain, the pain-ratio in male-female relationships may be closer than we think. There are more men than we realize, who have not yet recovered in spirit from the hurt initiated by a woman.

The inhibiting scents of a woman have origins which must be identified and adequately addressed and pruned. Like a bad odor in a refrigerator, if the origin is not found and discarded, it will permeate and spoil the rest of the food in the refrigerator. Inhibiting scents of a woman have permeated and spoiled many male-female relationships. Bad attitudes and a plethora of temperaments are just as pungent as inappropriate actions.

One of the most honorable acts that a woman can do to enhance her male-female relationship, is to acknowledge that she has inhibiting scents. If not, all of her male-female relationships will suffer.

Some inhibiting scents of a woman are directed toward their own sons. Mothers need to be conscious and careful that they are not dealing with their sons like they do men. I see this done too often. Some mothers have a hard time separating the two. Especially when some mothers have had not-so-positive experiences with men; now all males, even their sons, become the enemy.

Some mothers respond to their sons with the same negative spirit and attitude she has toward his father. If he is too much "like his daddy," transference goes on. It is not fair for these mothers to dump on their sons. It will certainly affect his mindset about women. The scent of negative *transference* inhibits many mother-son relationships. Unfortunately, his relationship with females - teachers, girlfriends, bosses, and his mother, will suffer. Transference wounds sons.

To be sure, mothers must be extremely careful of the scent they display toward their child's father. Inhibiting scents take a long time for the child to get that smell out of their olfactory brain.

I have a very keen interest in observing women in male-female relationships. Another inhibiting scent I occasionally detect is *manipulation*. Some women love to manipulate men. A lot of it is done in very subtle ways, and many men don't know they are being manipulated.

I grew up observing a ploy among many women that has been passed down from generation to generation. It is the belief that a woman must use manipulation to get her man to do what she desires. The real slick women have learned how to suggest something to their man in such a way that he thinks he is really the initiator of the suggestion. Many of you women know what I'm talking about. It's almost a rite of passage for some females to hone their skills in the subtle art of male manipulation.

Women give off an inhibiting scent when they are not upfront with their men. I don't have much respect for women who operate in this manner, and women who manipulate men don't have much respect for the men they manipulate. Its hard to respect someone you can manipulate. What these women need are servants, not husbands or boyfriends! Then, they won't have to scheme and manipulate them, they can just order them.

When a man sees a woman manipulate another man for her own self-interests, he immediately marks her as a woman not to be trusted. Also, her inhibiting scent of *manipulation* is quickly picked up by other men. They either avoid her or try to manipulate the manipulator.

Daily I see females running games on unsuspecting male victims. (Preying on naive males start early with some females. She knows she is not the least-bit interested in him, but she sees he can be hustled in some way, shape or form). These females are like a *venus fly-trap* flower - usually attractive and seductive - but deadly! They have caused untold mental and emotional hurt to countless men. Some men have gotten killed or killed themselves because of them.

Consequently, some mental-emotionally hurt males start reeking havoc on females, in reaction to the hurt they have been made to suffer. Some women help create abusers, stalkers, and the like! There is never any excuse for a male abusing, stalking, or retaliating, nor is there any excuse for a female to operate in such a way that precipitates the mental-emotional downfall of a male!

The sad reality is that many innocent women have reaped the brutal consequences (from men who have been mentally-emotionally hurt), what some guilty women have sown! And this is just the tip of the iceberg! If most men would come forward, they could reveal some of the most excruciating pain they have experienced from women in their male-female relationships. So much so, that much of the man-mending that many men desperately need, has a female in there some where, at the core of his pain!

There are very few experiences that can compare to the pain a man encounters from a woman. There are very few things a man won't do for a woman. You can count them on one hand. Some men will abrogate all of our Creator's natural and spiritual principles, just to appease a woman!

But when some men see that they have been duped, there is no limit to which they will go to even the score! Much of it depends upon the magnitude of the pain he has encountered. When women get disrespected or mistreated, including women who are not at fault, (although no disrespect or mistreatment of women is justifiable) it is oftentimes from men who have been weighted, wounded, oppressed or violated by a woman.

As I mentioned, some of the interruption of a man's spirit starts in the home with his mother. With other boys, it is with a female teacher in school. A lot of young men are put down in embarrassing ways by female peers and it registers in their spirit. The irony of this serious matter is that most of the girls, young ladies and women who weight, wound, oppress or violate a male's spirit have usually experienced the same interruption of spirit. It just surfaces in their relationships with their sons, male suitors, boyfriends and husbands. These actions are scents of a woman being released.

I don't have space to list all the inhibiting scents of a woman. I just want to share the three most inhibiting scents of a woman that I come in contact with on a regular basis in my counseling. They are, **unforgiveness**, **fear**, and **spirit depression**. In fact, they are more than scents. They are growths and formations that have been permitted to dominate and incarcerate the spirit of countless women.

It is my hope that something will be said to inspire women to acknowledge inhibiting growths and formations in their spirit and seek careful but necessary pruning.

Unforgiveness

Flower: **Snapdragon**: Snapdragons vary in color and fragrance. When the flower's petals, said to resemble the mouth of a dragon, are pulled apart and released, they close with an audible snap - hence the plant's name.

Scent: When fresh, snapdragons have a peculiar, heavy, disagreeable odor, which is in a great measure dissipated by drying, it has a weakly saline, bitter and slightly acrid taste.

I am certain that the majority of women who have been weighted, wounded, oppressed or violated want recovery and restoration of their spirit to a state of normalcy. But where do they start?

An initial incision must be made to open up a woman's interrupted spirit so she can begin the process of healing and wholeness. One of the first inhibiting growths that must be pruned out of many women's spirit is *unforgiveness.*

Forgiving those who weighted, wounded, oppressed or violated a woman's spirit can be a very painful thing to do. The fondling, molestation, rape, incest, and other hideous sexual crimes perpetrated against many females, are painful to think about, much less forgive.

Add to that list the physical, verbal, emotional abuse, neglect and desertion, where girls and young women became the brunt of their father's abuse or apathy, or anger from a male. It is not difficult to see why some women have difficulty forgiving those males, especially when those males have never expressed any remorse for committing such heinous acts!

Painful memories wear many women like a tight leather

skirt, especially when they see the male cousin, uncle, father or acquaintance that violated them. Even when some females have found the courage to confront them, most of those males get amnesia and say they don't remember or deny it ever happened!

Why in the world would a female come up to him and say he did this or that to her when she was young, for the fun of it? Those males know the females they violated, even repeatedly, but they don't or won't admit it because they can be subject to arrest and punishment.

So what does a sexually violated female do? Unless she has immediately reported it and gone to the hospital where she is examined, a report is taken, and semen or some other physical evidence is ascertained, and he matches the evidence, it is difficult for her to prove to the authorities who is the guilty one.

Most of these women live quietly but vividly, with those painful memories for years. Some are too ashamed to confide in others. But like a wrecking ball that continues to crash into a building, those ever-fresh memories continue to take a toll on the spirit of these women.

Unbeknownst to many women, but evident to others, are inhibiting scents that leak out, and these scents will continue to come forth until they are pruned out. I believe that hidden deep inside many women is the spirit of unforgiveness. It is a keepsake for some women, their only recourse, because they can't get back at their brutal violators.

Unforgiveness is one of the most inhibiting scents a woman can retain. Unforgiveness is one of the most repulsive scents that a woman can leave unpruned. Not only is unforgiveness inhibiting, it can become as pervasive as a skunk scent. In fact, unforgiveness will permeate every subsequent male-female relationship until it is addressed and resolved.

Unforgiveness is an unhealthy spirit that roots in the inner-most sanctum of a woman's being. When unforgiveness finds residency in a woman's spirit, it gradually takes over a woman's soul - her thoughts, emotions and will.

Her *thoughts* become fixated in her past, making it more difficult for her to be optimistic about any future male-female relationships. A plethora of unhealthy *emotions* keep her in an unending cycle of pain, anger, or bitterness, although many women mask it well. Her *will*, which is pivotal to her restoration, slowly relinquishes its power to root out this unforgiveness so she can move on with her life.

Consequently, her body, that is, her mental and/or physical health, is usually affected in various ways. Without excising this unhealthy formation from her spirit, a woman may live the rest of her life in pain. But praise be to our Creator! There is an antidote if she wishes to finally be set free! It's called, *forgiveness*.

As unacceptable and inexcusable as these male or female violators are, they still need to be forgiven. They need forgiveness more than they even realize. Until they are forgiven, they cannot be set free. Please understand what I mean. Forgiveness does not mean they should not be held responsible for their wrong-doing, because they should, and they will. It might not be in a court of law, but all violators will reap, in some way or another, what they have sown. That's a natural and spiritual principle that can never be changed.

Forgiveness may begin a restoration of spirit within both victim and violator. Something wrong has happened within the spirit of violators who commit inexcusable acts, as well as within the victim who refuses to forgive. Forgiveness has a way of freeing both to reach out for help and hope.

Forgiveness does not absolve violators of their wrong-doing. Forgiveness, like no other conscious decision, actually provides them with an atmosphere and opportunity to acknowledge, confess and rectify their wrong-doing.

But unless the victim is willing to forgive, their spirit will remain closed. Forgiveness opens the spirit and gives both victim and violator the opportunity to release all that has accumulated over the years.

Someone once said, "The most noble form of vengeance is forgiveness." If you really want revenge, forgive them! If you really, really want to make them pay for all your hurt and pain, forgive them!

What some men did was so despicable that some of you feel you can't forgive them. They don't deserve it. Some of you wish the worst on them. That's understandable. But that posture doesn't liberate you. It keeps your spirit incarcerated. It keeps you locked in your past. And as long as you take the position of unforgiveness, you are consigning your own spirit to a life sentence!

I wish I could be more explicit so that some of you women can see your reality for what it is. You hold the key to your recovery and restoration of spirit! As long as you resist forgiving your wrong-doer, you will not be restored in spirit, soul or body.

Forgiveness is the initial incision that actually begins the pruning process in your spirit. Just as the incision in the plant begins the pruning process, so forgiveness begins the process of restoration of spirit. If you have been weighted, wounded, oppressed or violated by a man, whether in childhood, youth or adulthood, you may begin the recovery and restoration of a normal spirit by forgiving them.

What forgiving does is, open your spirit to be pruned, so that a new spirit and a new life can come forth. That's your decision alone. Anyway, aren't you tired? Doesn't your spirit need restoring? Don't you want to be free?

Let's reverse it so you can view the spirit-releasing power of forgiveness better. Have you ever done someone wrong? When you went to them to make it right and they forgave you, what did it do for you? It freed you from the burden of guilt or shame. Now you didn't have to dodge them any-more. You could look them straight in the eye. Why? Because you were forgiven. Your burden was pruned.

Forgiving the wrong-doer frees you from being a victim. You will remain a victim as long as you choose not to forgive them. When you forgive, you stop being a victim and you can embark upon the road to becoming a victor! Why? Because you are free to do so.

Victims remain victims as long as they refuse to let go of their victimization. Victims can become whole in spirit again! Although it does not happen over-night, you can will to move from victim-to-victor!

Forgiveness is a spiritual dynamic. This might be the most important point. Forgiveness can only come via the spirit. Someone said, "To err is human, to forgive is divine." That's true. Forgiveness is a divine attribute, a divine gift given by our Creator to erring humans to restore weighted, wounded, oppressed and violated spirits - the very place that has been interrupted in your male-female relationships.

Some painful experiences in male-female relationships are lodged so deep in a woman's spirit that only forgiveness can dislodge them. Women who are open to and guided by our Creator's Spirit will forgive. They may not have any positive feelings for the man, but forgiveness is not based on how one feels. It's about freedom from an interrupted spirit.

Like a crushed flower, the spirit of a woman who is willing to look up to our Creator for the strength to forgive, will receive the strength to forgive. Besides, all of us have erred. Because we have, we all stand in need of being forgiven by someone. Then we need to forgive.

Forgiveness is not only for healing; it's also for restoration. Unforgiveness is self-bondage. If your spirit has been interrupted by a man or woman and you refuse to forgive them, you will not function in a state of normalcy. Now, it is not what they have done in the past that will keep you bound, but your unwillingness to unlock yourself from your past, plan your recovery strategy in the present, and move in faith toward your glorious future.

Forgiveness brings closure. After an incision and the extraction of growths and formations on the spirit, there must be closure. *These spirit-interrupting experiences and encounters will have to be referred to as closed chapters in a woman's life.* You should not keep rehashing what happened to you. Without closure, wounds stay fresh and subject to further infection. Forgiveness is the best way to initiate closure. Forgiveness says its over. So many women need closure now. Forgive and move on.

If I could give you a more complete way of getting your spirit open for healing and restoration, I would not hesitate. But I know no other way to begin abundant living than forgiveness. I know because I have had to forgive others, and I have had to be forgiven. I can only conclude that forgiveness is the most thorough and complete divine and conscious decision that brings the most lasting results for the offended and their offenders.

Permit me to repeat something I said earlier because it is important to reiterate: *Understanding why, when and how to prune will help produce healthy, strong and productive plants.* Although I mentioned that forgiveness is the initial incision that opens a woman's spirit to restoration, as well as the action that initiates closure, understanding the facets of forgiveness helps us understand the *why* of pruning.

The *when* of the pruning process will vary from woman-to-woman. Because the interruptions of spirit take on different reactions and results for women who have been weighted, wounded, oppressed or violated, only that woman can say when her pruning process should begin.

Situations and circumstances, too numerous to recount, make the *when* for some women immediate, but for others, eventual. For instance, a girl who is being molested by a male should report it immediately. But because of threats of physical harm to herself or a family member by the violator, she is afraid to tell. Oftentimes, the molestation goes on for years, until she musters up the courage to say "when." It could be when she feels physically safe enough to divulge his wrong-doing or when she refuses to suffer any more.

One woman I counseled with said she continued to be abused so that the violator would not start abusing her younger sister. Telling a female that she should have reported it right away is the right thing to do, and may be the ideal, but sometimes, not her reality.

How many women have stayed in abusive male-female relationships for the sake of their children? How about those females who feel too ashamed to let someone know what has been going on? I just can't speak for women on this point, but I do encourage them to say *when* !

What women in bad male-female relationships need is some kind of support system. Today, there is an endless list of local and national support systems for women for all kinds of violations against them. Many local resources can be contacted through toll free 1-800 numbers. A viable support system is quintessential for a woman who seeks recovery and restoration of spirit. Then pruning, while painful at times, has a supportive environment for women.

How the pruning process takes place will also vary from woman-to-woman. The *how* has to do with the type of intervention a woman will seek. As I mentioned in *Smellin' Ourselves: What Men Need To Understand About Ourselves And Our Women,* the intervention must be truthful, principled and solution-oriented to obtain lasting results.

How a woman should approach her recovery and restoration of spirit may be through individual, marital or family counseling, therapy, support groups, reading, seminars, or whatever appropriate and adequate resource is within her ability to secure.

Summation

In the divine order of human existence, our Creator's Spirit within our human spirit is to direct our soul, that is, our thoughts, emotions, will, and our body is to be the servant to carry out its directives.

When humans don't cooperate with our Creator's natural and spiritual principles, women (and men) are more vulnerable to the interruption of spirit, *dis-ease* of spirit.

Although environment may play a part in the enhancing or inhibiting of a woman's spirit, it is primarily the transmission of weights, wounds, oppression or violations, from person-to-person that results in so much loss for women. So many women with so much potential and ability, have lost valuable and productive years, and for some women, their lives, because of a male's ignorance or disregard of our Creator's natural and spiritual principles.

The *why*, *when* and *how* of pruning are essential to the present and future growth and direction of women in need of addressing, resolving and moving on to abundant living.

I am not saying that all women will start by forgiving their offenders. That may take some time for some women. *I simply want to emphasize that recovery and restoration of a woman's spirit back to a state of normalcy cannot be accomplished without forgiveness being some part of the process. The spirit of bitterness, resentment, hatred, anger, and the like, will never lift weights, close wounds, liberate the oppressed or restore the violated spirits of women.* None of them have the ability to bring closure.

Besides, if you have ever gotten a "whiff" of a woman who has an unforgiving spirit, just her pungent scent ought to be incentive for us to pray for a forgiving spirit. **No new real growth will take place until unforgiveness is removed from her spirit.**

But for the women who are "sick and tired of being sick and tired" of an interrupted spirit, pruning unforgiveness relieves the burden on their spirit; enhances the quality of their lives; encourages mental and emotional health; and helps reshape their future male-female relationships. Aren't these results worth pruning unforgiveness? I think so.

Fear

Flower: **Amaryllis**: A tender, flowering bulb. The word actually means "sparkling" and refers to the attractive bloom. Given the proper treatment, the amaryllis will continue to bloom for several years, usually in winter.

Scent: Amaryllis bulbs that are not cultivated right will flower slow and with less stems. Some will probably not flower at all. To restore, amaryllis needs plenty of warmth, water and food. Take care not to damage new shoots. If properly cared for, the bulbs should increase in size each year.

"There is no fear in love. Matured love casts out fear, because fear torments. The person who fears is not matured in love.[1]

Fear torments, as the Scripture says. The definition of torment is, "great pain or anguish; to agitate or upset greatly; to annoy or harass." Fear is a tormentor! Fear is an interrupter of love. It is difficult for a male-female relationship to flourish if a woman has unresolved fears.

In my book, *Family Matters: Hope and Healing*, I talk about fear. Let me share some of it with you:

"Fear is wrestling. Fear is tiring, too. Fear may be the biggest impediment to healing. So many people have a fear of rejection, fear of failure, fear of intimacy, fear of the truth, etc. Fear is an emotion fueled by a desire to avoid pain or keep from being harmed; yet, fear has done more to immobilize hope and healing than any other enemy, except death.

[1] 1 John 4:18

So many people embrace fear, not recognizing that fear is our enemy. Fear is against us, not for us. By harboring fear, we are harboring the archenemy of hope and healing. Think about it. We are harboring, feeding and housing our enemy!"

Fear is a decision. It takes something stronger than fear to be liberated from it. Mba Mbulu said, *"Fear is one of the most natural emotions. Therefore, no one can be blamed or ridiculed for responding to a threatening situation in a fearful manner. However, there are times when it is necessary to control your response to fear, to analyze what is causing the fear and determine if the risk to your health or security, or whatever, is worth enduring."*[2]

I believe that Brother Mbulu's assessment of fear is accurate. Fear is not something a woman necessarily invites. In this case, fear is generally a natural response to a threatening situation in male-female relationships. Fear certainly interrupts a woman's spirit, soul and body, inhibiting normalcy.

But Brother Mbulu insists that fear should not get carte blanche, that is, unrestricted access. There is a healthy fear and an unhealthy fear. Consequently, one needs " to analyze what is causing the fear and determine if the risk to your health or security is worth enduring." Mbulu gives sound counsel that should be heeded.

Any fear that inhibits spirit, soul or body from functioning in a state of normalcy is an unhealthy fear. But how is unhealthy fear sown? Some fears females take into womanhood, marriage and family have their source in childhood experiences. The acronym F.E.A.R. means, **F**alse **E**ducation **A**ccepted as **R**eality.

To a great extent, some women did not receive proper and

[2] Mba Mbulu, Black-Smart

accurate information concerning males when they were young. They grew up with a distorted concept of manhood. The not-so-positive experiences with a father, or some other male, distorted their perceptions about males. In all spheres of education, there is true and false. A falsehood believed becomes reality to the person.

Continuing from the previous chapter, since a father is to be a girl's first positive male relationship, to an extent, fathers set the example as it relates to males in general. Permit me to quote again from my book, *Family Matters: Hope and Healing*, about the father-daughter relationship:

"Fathers establishing a wholesome, loving relationship with their daughters from birth is of utmost importance. Girls need their fathers to gain a proper concept of manhood first-hand. They need him to be a spiritual, moral, wise, patient guide in her life. A father doesn't have to be perfect to be principled. If our daughters have that, they have a distinctive advantage, especially in relationships with men later in life.

The father-daughter relationship is something to be considered in dating and marriage. It doesn't have to be the deciding factor, but an honest consideration. Understanding the thoughts and views of a female concerning men is important. If she didn't get a healthy concept of manhood from her father or a positive male influence in her upbringing, it is important for a male admirer to know how she thinks concerning men and how her thought processes evolved to her present thinking.

She can develop a healthy and balanced view of manhood without a father in the home, but she can't develop it without some positive male influence in her life at some time in her development - even if it is from reading the biographies of strong, principled, compassionate, women-respecting men. She has to have envisioned this kind of man, in some way, before it can be a part of her reality and her life.

The father-daughter relationship has volumes to do with male-female relationships. When fathers treat their daughters with unconditional love and respect, while affirming their individuality, they learn to appreciate and discern men who love and respect them, and are not threatened by their individuality."[3]

In the case of the absent father complex, many fathers have robbed their own daughters of a most important essential at the most important time in their developing years: A loving, spiritual, principled father!

As in the case of **J**, and so many other women, these distorted concepts have created a host of fears, still alive that inhibit their male-female relationships. Add to them all the women who have had encounters or experiences with males, other than their fathers, who have weighted, wounded, oppressed or violated them in spirit, soul or body. Is it any wonder that fear rules in some women's lives?

Every fear has its source or root in spirit. Fear is without a doubt, a spirit. It is a spirit of fear. This means we are dealing with an activating or essential principle in the innermost being of a person. But it is a woman's thoughts, emotions and will that gives fear its longevity and dominance.

Fear viciously attacks her thoughts, emotions and will - that is her volition, our decision-making faculty. It is her thinking that affects her emotions or feelings, and then she usually responds or behaves accordingly. Thus, fear has a painful way of tormenting her, especially when she has not-so-positive encounters in male-female relationships, beginning in childhood. It is from this impetus that fear has a way of causing a woman to withhold herself, she being a com-

3 Kwame Ronnie Vanderhorst, Family Matters: Hope and Healing

posite of her thoughts, emotions and will. Let's go back to **J** for clarity.

J's thoughts and emotions were so overwhelmed by her father's misdeeds that she willed not to let any man weight, wound, oppress or violate her. But to do this, she had to withhold herself. She willed not to be vulnerable in any way to a man, decreasing her chances of getting hurt. **J** closed her thought process and steeled her emotions. No man would ever see her sweat!

In short, **J**'s deepest thoughts were withheld from males, including her husband and son. To my knowledge, she had never divulged her underlying thoughts she had acquired about males, that prompted her actions or reactions with her husband or son. She is withholding a fundamental part of herself that would bring immediate clarity to her husband and son. Then, they could reflect back and understand why she said, did and acted the way she did.

In the same vein, **J** has withheld her emotions. She has yet to feel free enough to take her guard down. Even though her father may have been the cause, her husband and son have felt the effect. **J** reminds me of the story of the female elephant who was placed behind a fence when she was born. Years later, as a full grown elephant, she still stood behind that same fence. People wondered aloud, "Why doesn't that elephant just walk over that small fence?" The keeper simply replied, "Because she has been conditioned that she cannot go outside of that fence."

J, and so many other women, have conditioned themselves to believe they can't live without their fears. Although they don't call them fears, they feel letting down their guard would leave them more vulnerable.

But vulnerability should be the least of their concerns. By "analyzing and determining the risks to their health" they will discover that unhealthy fears can cause a chemical imbalance and make them susceptible to illness and disease.

In releasing fear, **J** may experience a new capacity to fully give of herself. **J** can learn to love without reservation. **J** would release a new, enhancing scent into the atmosphere of her marriage and family! She would also be set free from the torment that accompanies fear!

Fear must be pruned. If there is to be a recovery and restoration of your spirit, soul and body to a state of normalcy, pruning fear is not an option; it is a necessity. But it is not best that you do this pruning by yourself. Plants don't prune themselves. Someone else does that. The plant just cooperates fully. You need help with the pruning process.

Pruning is my way of saying that a principled, solution-oriented intervention is the best way of getting to the root of your fears. Refusing to prune is to allow the growths and formations that inhibit your male-female relationships to become terminal. But you must have a good reason, a proper motivation, to cooperate with the pruning process. *Love* is that reason, your purest motivation.

The antidote for fear is love. Love evicts fear. The more you love, the less you fear. But some of you may ask, "How do I love?" Let me distinguish the love I am referring to in the pruning of fear. There are three basic understandings of love. *Eros*, is a sexual love. This type of love may be selfish. It cannot fulfill the needs of a woman's spirit, nor can it guarantee a mutually fulfilling relationship.

The second type of love is *Phileo*. Phileo love is a brotherly or sisterly love, affection or kindness toward someone. The word philanthropist comes from this root, phileo. It also denotes a kindly act of love for the betterment of humankind. As honorable as phileo love is, it is still not the type of love that can uproot fears.

The love that I am referring to is, *Agape*. This is the love our Creator has bestowed upon humanity. My Expository Dictionary of New Testament Words defines our Creator's agape love: *"It expresses the deep and constant love and interest of a perfect Being towards entirely unworthy objects, producing and fostering a reverential love in them towards the Giver, and a practical love toward those who are partakers of the same, and a desire to help others to seek the Giver."*[4]

This is the type of love that is necessary for one to learn to love themselves and others properly. Agape love has more to do with our *will* and *attitude* than it does with our feelings. Agape love is not dependent upon accompanying feelings to be effective. It functions regardless of feelings, regardless of how you feel about others or yourself. **Agape love is an unconditional love, a will and attitude of the highest regard for yourself and others, with no strings attached.**

Our human love is conditional. I can understand that. It's usually based on our experiences and encounters in life. That is why we need a divine love that transcends our human experiences and gives us the freedom to love ourselves and others without meeting some rigid criteria.

Eros or sexual love does not fulfill our deepest longings and desires. Phileo love is good and has its place in serving humanity, but it cannot bring to closure the nagging fears that bind us and keep us from mutually fulfilling male-female relationships.

Agape love can inspire the fearful to walk over their fence and move on in life. This is how agape love works: Agape love is not predicated upon a person's behavior as to whether they deserve our love. Agape love is a will and atti-

[4] W. E. Vine, Expository Dictionary of New Testament Word

tude that seeks to do what is in one's best interest, regardless of their past or present wrong-doing. Agape love functions, not based on feelings, but on divine principles.

When a woman has been weighted, wounded, oppressed or violated, agape love empowers her to forgive her wrong-doer, and by doing so, she frees herself from being a victim. She steps over the fence from victim to victor! She has finally won! Although the wrong-doer may be entirely unworthy, the agape love shown toward him or her is a seed planted in them that now has the ability to begin to transform their life.

It is not a small thing in the mind of a wrong-doer to be forgiven by his victim. That's mind-boggling, knowing he or she is totally unworthy of forgiveness. Only through agape love can forgiveness be extended to a wrong-doer. Agape love is divine love given to transform one's life.

But agape love doesn't stop there. From then on, the wrong-doer is treated as if he has never committed any wrong! I am not telling you something I think you should do. I am presently extending agape love to some people who have done me wrong. This wisdom and instruction is for me too! I had to prune some resentment out of me, and now I'm just sharing the process with you.

Agape love does not hold the wrong against the wrong-doer anymore. That does not mean you forget what they have done, because you never will. But agape love that is bestowed upon them means you will, if necessary, and within reason and your ability, do what is in their best interest, health and well-being.

Let me give you an example of agape love in action. I have a friend who told me her experience. She was divorced. The marriage had not been good, to say it kindly. Her former husband is the father of her two children. He remarried. That marriage went bad, he had no place to live, and he was in a bad way. He called his first wife and asked if he could come and stay there until he got himself together. Now enough had gone on between them in their marriage for her to emphatically say, "No!" But she considered her sons - his sons too - and the time they could have with him. So in agape love, she let him come.

She regarded her sons, as well as her ability to assist her former husband. Her decision was not based upon her feelings or their rocky past, but upon the principle of the whole situation. Things worked out fine, and he left in a very reasonable time. Plus, her sons were able to see agape love in action. Their mother did what was within reason and her ability, and what was in the best interest and well-being of everyone involved.

The agape love she showed set her free! It enabled her to face her former husband and their past, not with malice, but with a dignity and a divine response that defies human reasoning. She has truly brought closure to a painful past and fears, by opening herself to love on a higher principle. Agape love evicted her fear. She crossed over her fence. She's free! Without responding from agape love, she would still be bound by her past experiences with her former husband. Her sons have renewed their relationship with their father. They talk often and visit each other periodically.

One more thing about agape love: **Not only does it consider and act in the best, principled, interest of others, it also has everything to do with you loving yourself**. The Scripture said, "There is no fear in love. Perfected love casts out fear." This word, *perfected* means, complete, fully grown or mature. This is a love that has grown or matured beyond eros and phileo. This is complete love, not conditional love. Agape love inspires love for ourselves, doing what is within reason and our ability, and what is in our own best interest and well-being. Agape love does not always say, "Yes." When it is in our own best interest, health and well-being, agape love may say, "No."

Women will never "get over the fence" of fear if they don't extend agape love to themselves. You deserve a healthy regard for yourself that causes you to do what is right and best for yourself.

I like what Henry H. Mitchell intimates about loving yourself. Mitchell says agape love is not the same as self-centered love. He goes on to say that love for our Creator, our neighbor and ourselves is inseparable. Without a healthy love - acceptance and regard for ones own self - it's difficult to love our Creator and others.[5]

This means, no matter how you feel about yourself, or how you were made to feel about yourself, based on your past not-so-positive experiences, you can still choose to place your health and well-being ahead of your feelings. Doing this shows you truly do love yourself.

I will end with Mbulu's wisdom and counsel: "*Fear is one of the most natural emotions. Therefore, no one can be blamed or ridiculed for responding to a threatening situation in a fearful manner. However, there are times when it is necessary to control your response to fear; to analyze what is causing the fear and determine if the risk to your health or security (or whatever) is worth enduring.*"

No unhealthy fear is worth the risk to your health and happiness. Replace your fears with agape love. You're worth it!

[5] H. M. Mitchell and E.M. Thomas, Preaching for Black Self Esteem

Facing Your Fears

1. What are your three primary fears that has plagued you in your male-female relationship? List them:

a. ______________________________

b. ______________________________

c. ______________________________

2. Who and what caused your primary fears? List the person's initials and write the cause of your primary fears.

a. ______________________________

b. ______________________________

c. ______________________________

3. Have you confronted the person(s) in any way concerning the fears they have caused? Yes No

4. Have you sought and found principled, solution-oriented intervention to resolve your fears? Yes No

5. Have you forgiven them for their wrong-doing against you? Yes No. If "No," why not?

____

____

6. If you haven't forgiven them, are you willing to forgive them for their wrong-doing against you? Yes No. If "No," why not?

____

____

____

Spirit Depression

Flower: **Clematis**: As a member of the buttercup family, this vine-like flower varies in form, color and height. Clematis are generally hardy plants and have been known to survive for 25 years or more.

Scent: Threatened by a virulent fungal infestation knows as "clematis wilt." Unable to summon defense mechanism to counter the invasion by the fungi, stem wilts. It is assumed that the clematis is dead. The correct action is to gently explore the top half inch of soil around the stem. Will usually find that the roots are already sending up shoots. This means the plant is still alive and needs care. If no shoots are apparent, continue special care, especially watering of the plant and shoots will soon appear.

I would be remiss if I didn't address one of the most pervasive and predominant scents that is indicative of many women's spirit today. It is depression. I have never seen so many woman so depressed in all my life! Certainly, spirit depression is not a new phenomenon among women or men. It just seems to be more prevalent than a few years ago.

There are women-galore, who are succumbing to spirit depression, yet, it is hid well by many women. Much of their spirit depression is submerged beneath Revelon cosmetics, Ann Klein suits, Mervis diamonds, Victoria's Secret, Haines stockings, and Nine West shoes, but it's there.

The pressures of society, family and relationships, have the ability to overwhelm a woman. Many women are survivors. Some women are tough as nails. Some women stay afloat while living in denial. Some women have various coping mechanisms that work for them. But toughness, denial and coping can expend a woman's energy, and then what? Get tougher? More denial? Another coping tactic? It is obvious that a spirit-depressed woman cannot function in a state of normalcy.

Depression is a spirit. Any spirit, be it healthy or unhealthy, first affects our human spirit. Since our spirit is the activating or essential principle of our whole being, depression affects the core of our being. When the human spirit is interrupted by an unhealthy spirit, our thoughts, emotions and will are overwhelmed, our body is inevitably affected.

Spirit depression is toxic. The principles our Creator encoded in nature causes nature to be reciprocal and cooperative, unless something upsets nature's balance. For instance, the earth is reciprocal and cooperative to provide food for human consumption and existence. When a toxic substance gets put into the earth, such as dioxin, it reeks havoc upon plant, animal and human life.

In the exact same way, our Creator made our spirit to govern and cooperate with our soul and body. Since the spirit, soul and body are interdependent, what affects one, affects the other. When our spirit is toxic, that is, interrupted or infiltrated by an unhealthy occupant, it reeks havoc upon our soul and body.

Spirit depression is toxic. It infiltrates the whole human being. Spirit depression spreads like toxin, slowly but surely, until the whole person is overwhelmed. Mental, emotional, and oftentimes, physical health problems may result.

Spirit depression is a state of being. The dictionary defines depression as the "state of being depressed; disorder marked by sadness, inactivity, difficulty in thinking and concentration, and feelings of dejection." (I'm not addressing clinical depression, just spirit depression).

There are factors that may cause spirit depression. I don't even know most of them. I can only cite causes that I believe occur when some women succumb to spirit depression. I have observed two fountainheads that flow into many tributaries that may lead to spirit depression: *unfulfilled and unrealistic expectations.*

The expectations of most woman are similar, yet, dissimilar. A very short list of the most basic of similarities are the desire for love, protection, respect and equality. How they expect to receive them may bring dissimilarity among most women.

Unfulfilled Expectations

To be sure, men are not always certain how most women expect to receive fulfillment in their male-female relationships. That's why men must understand that adequate and complete communication is as vital as breathing for women in male-female relationships. A man should not be ashamed for not knowing, but he should be ashamed for not asking.

On the other hand, many women expect a men to know, without asking, how to fulfill their expectations. Just by some men asking some women what do they need, can get some men in hot water, because some women expect them to already know what they expect in order to be fulfilled!

When it comes to many women getting depressed in spirit because of not having their expectations fulfilled in their male-female relationships, some of it has to do with some men's lack of understanding of their woman's needs versus her wants.

A man with a distorted concept of womanhood, based

upon a faulty male socialization, blurs the line of demarcation between a woman's wants and her needs. Unfortunately, many men are socialized to believe that women want "things." Things make her happy. Some men just don't know what women need. Again, much of it can be traced back to his socialization as a boy and youth.

Women have a diversity of wants, and those wants are just as diverse as women. It is said that "diamonds are a girl's best friend." There are women who are not into jewelry. Others want all the gold and diamonds a man can give them. They feel "naked" without jewelry. Some women refuse to ride in certain kinds of cars with men. Other women could care less, are just glad not to have to walk. It can be challenging for a man to fulfill a woman's wants.

As I stated, the diversity of wants of women are as diverse as women, but there are only a few things a woman needs in order to live an abundant life. All a woman needs is love, respect, protection and equality, and she will be fulfilled. Of course, appropriate actions accompany each of those needs.

When a man doesn't understand spirit, what it is, its function, and its centrality in male-female relationships, he may confuse a woman's wants with her needs. Protracted unfulfillment of her needs may cause her to become depressed in her spirit.

Faulty male socialization has conditioned men to think that materialism, success, upper mobility, fame, and a host of other accouterments, can fulfill a woman. To be fair, it is not difficult for women to get caught up in confusing their needs with their wants. But when reality sets in, most women still find themselves unfulfilled. Spirit depression may not be far behind.

Probably the greatest unfulfilled expectation that may cause some women spirit-depression is when her man sets his sights lower than his true potential. There are no perfect men. But women do expect the men they are in a relationship with to be all that he has ability to be. No excuses.

I may have said this earlier, but it bears repeating. **Most men date or marry the woman they want. But most women date and marry the man in whom they see potential in. What becomes depressing is when the man never realizes or reaches the potential his woman sees in him.** So many women are still waiting for their man to not only realize his potential, but to access it. That can be depressing.

Reaching his potential has less to do with pay, position or prestige. It has all to do with a man understanding his Creator-given potential, and discovering how to develop and utilize that potential to its fullest. If pay, position or prestige is the byproduct of maximizing his potential, so be it. Our Creator be praised!

Male-female relationships have a difficult time being mutually fulfilling when a man fails to maximize or reach his potential. Some men show discomfort and sometimes envy when a woman he loves excels above him.

When a man places the wants of a woman before her true needs, or when he continuously falls short of realizing and/or reaching his potential, spirit depression may result in her from her unfulfilled expectations in their male-female relationship.

Unrealistic Expectations

Unrealistic expectations may cause spirit depression for some women. Traditional male-female relationships assume that the man is is going to meet all of her physical, mental-emotional, spiritual, social and economic expectations. Now that's a long row for any man to hoe!

So much pressure is put on men by some women that they feel strangled at times. I call it the "Eve complex." In the Genesis narrative, Eve had all she needed, but she wanted more, and when she got what she wanted, she lost what she had! It cannot be denied that some men are losing good women. But it is equally true that some women are losing good men because of their unrealistic expectations. Like Eve, much of it has to do with their, "lust of the flesh, the lust of her eyes and the pride of life."[1]

It is true that some women have prioritized their wants above their needs. Women who prioritize their wants above their needs place themselves in a position to be unfulfilled in life. Should their man not fulfill their multitudinous wants, it becomes difficult for them to keep their spirit from sinking into depression.

When I was growing up, these women were known as, "golddiggers." In the 80's, they became, "material girls." It is too irreverent to repeat what they are called in the 90's! But for all intents and purposes, women (and men) with unrealistic expectations are very unhappy in their male-female relationships.

Happiness is relative, and its ability to provide total fulfillment, improbable. *Happiness is where you find it, but rarely where you seek it.* This consumer-driven society has an uncanny and calculated way of equating happiness with material acquisition. It's this simple: "Get it and you will be happy." Happiness is elusive.

Yet, that's a difficult sell for women with unrealistic expectations. They have taken the bait that they can be fulfilled in male-female relationships from the outside-in. The truth is, most women find personal fulfillment from the inside-out. That's also how they find true fulfillment in their

[1] 1 John 2:15-17

male-female relationships. That's what women need to know if they expect mutual fulfillment in male-female relationships.

Let me suggest that a woman is not dependent upon a man to be fulfilled at each stage of her life, be it personal, professional or relational. If her spirit is rightly attended to. This decreases her spirit depression.

I want to show you a diagram that is in my book, *Smellin' Ourselves: What Men Need To Understand About Ourselves And Our Women.* Women need to know the divine order of human existence, and how to truly become fulfilled within.

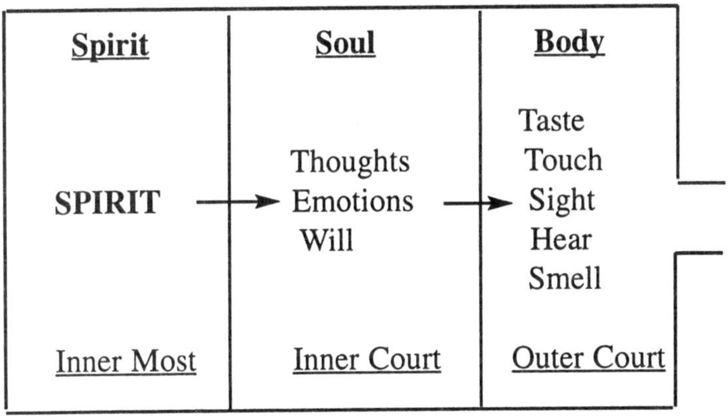

The Scripture says, "What? Don't you know your body is the temple of our Creator's Holy Spirit?[2] The writer seems to be filled with amazement by beginning his question with, "What?" He is inferring, "Hasn't anyone told you this?" "Your parents never informed you?" The truth is that most girls were not instructed in this sacred reality, so they never knew that our Creator is to be "honored in their body and spirit."

"If you don't understand spirit, what it is, its function,

[2] 1 Corinthians 6:19-20

and its centrality in male-female relationships, everything else you think you understand about male-female relationships will only confuse you."

Our spirit is to be the control center of our lives and relationships. We were created to live and love from center-to-circumference - from the inside-out. Men and women were not created to be controlled by the desires of their bodies. We all know people who have made a mess of their lives by catering to the dictates of their bodily desires.

Men and women were not created to be ruled by their souls. Our soul is the home of our thoughts, emotions and will. The soul can function without truthful information and spiritual instruction, and that is dangerous. Neither did our Creator intend for our soul to function independently.

We were created to live and love on a higher spiritual plateau with our *spirit. Our spirit is to direct our soul, and our body is to be its servant, carrying out its directions.* This is the divine order of human existence for life and relationships.

When we bring this understanding of the divine order of human existence into the context of unfulfilled and unrealistic expectations that can lead to spirit depression, we may find the reasons why there is so much unfulfillment in male-female relationships.

I believe that a lot of spirit depression experienced by many women has to do with the futile attempts of men to cater to the desires of a woman's body and soul instead of attending the needs of her spirit. The desire for physical and emotional satisfaction supersedes the needs of many women's spirit. Sooner or later, spirit depression sets in.

Men must learn that the so-called intangibles in the male-female relationship can fulfill his wife or woman, more than the tangible or visible things. Intangibles, such as, a man's active support and involvement with his children, occasional expressions of appreciation, regular participation in home chores, romantic expressions and surprises, trustworthiness, taking some time each day for intimate communications, private and public chivalrous deportment, an optimistic outlook on life, personal, intellectual and career development, active listening, a willingness to readily admit wrongs and sincere apologies, supporting her wholesome endeavors, and I could go on and on.

It is difficult for a man to fulfill his woman from the outside-in. True fulfillment is from the inside-out. Consequently, so many men are confused and so many women are depressed. And vice versa.

When a woman's spirit is at the mercy of the thoughts and emotions, or her innate bodily desires, there is no telling how low her spirit may sink into the abyss of discouragement, despair and depression.

When a woman's spirit is in ascendency, she is in a position to be most fulfilled. When her spirit is submerged and her body or soul is given ascendency, that's when she may be most unfulfilled and depressed in her spirit.

The spirit cannot be placed beneath the body and soul and not be depressed. Spirit depression comes from giving priority or ascendency to the soul or body over the spirit.

When men and women learn how to attend each other's spirit first, then fulfillment in soul and body becomes the byproduct. This is what I call a "mutually-fulfilling" male-female relationship.

Mutual Fulfillment

Mutual fulfillment in male-female relationships begins with the spirit. Since our spirit is the activating and essential principle of our whole being, it is to be governed by our

Creator's Spirit within our human spirit. We must ask our Creator to place in our spirit the Holy Spirit.

When our spirit becomes the residence of our Creator's Spirit, there are spiritual activities that can keep our spirit in ascendency, counteract depression, encourage mutual fulfillment, and enhance male-female relationships.

Just as our body and soul have specific functions, so does our spirit. The functions or activities of our spirit are to be *spiritual* and uplifting in nature. When our spirit is interrupted, without personal perseverance in retaining spirit ascendency, these spiritual activities may be surrendered or terminated.

Here are the spiritual activities that keep our spirit in ascendency, counteract depression, encourage mutual fulfillment, and enhance male-female relationships:

Worship is an activity of the spirit. I am not referring to religion, although religion can be included. Worship is an ongoing belief, practice or activity in which an individual chooses to honor the Creator.

Praise to our Creator is an activity of our spirit. I've already commented on praise as an enhancing, spiritual activity.

Prayer, which is a way of communicating with our Creator, is a very important function of the spirit. We can communicate our cares and concerns, our plans and petitions, in faith, believing that we will be heard by our Creator, and answers provided in our Creator's own time and way.

Fellowship is an activity of our spirit. Nothing in creation exists unto itself. Just as our Creator made us for relationships, we were also made for fellowship with one another. Fellowship is a specific reason that people of kindred spirits come together to communicate, disseminate information, wholesome socialization, and uplifting endeavors. It is difficult to maintain a strong spiritual life apart from fellowship with others.

The Word - truthful information and spiritual instruction, is an activity of our spirit. Without study, discussion and making truthful information and spiritual instruction a part of one's daily living, there will be no spiritual growth. Not only can the Word be a part of one's Fellowship, it should also be a part of one's personal study life.

If a woman's personal life or male-female relationship excludes worship, praise, prayer, fellowship, and reception of truthful information and spiritual instruction, she will lack personal or mutual fulfillment.

Just as our body needs physical exercise, and our soul needs mental stimulation and healthy emotions, so our spirit needs attention. Without these activities of the spirit, our spirit will be depressed.

A woman has the best chance of having her expectations fulfilled in male-female relationships when she has a man who not only understands spirit, but engages together in the spiritual activities that keep the spirit fresh, hopeful, and encouraged. Likewise, a woman has a better chance of fulfilling her man when she understands spirit and engages in personal spiritual activities that keeps her spirit ascended above the wants and needs of her soul and body.

If in your male-female relationships you have no interest or participation in spiritual activities, mutual fulfillment may be as elusive as a butterfly.

Men or women who have a low-to-no interest in spiritual activities, usually have a high interest in physical gratification, material, and even intellectual acquisition. Daily, I counsel "successful failures." They are successful by the standards of society, but a failure in personal, relational and spiritual life.

Summation

In the final analysis, it is the state of your spirit that will profoundly affect your personal and/or relational fulfillment or unfulfillment. Ultimately, you have the final say-so, as it pertains to spirit depression or spirit ascendency.

Spirit depression can be minimized and eliminated. That does not mean your spirit will not be interrupted at times, because it will. It all has to do with understanding spirit, its function and its centrality in your personal and male-female relationships.

Enhancing Scents Of A Woman

I don't know one man who doesn't want his woman to smell good. The enhancing scents of a woman will turn most men's heads quickly. I've even seen men follow a woman with a sweet-smelling scent through the mall!

When a woman's spirit has been pruned of its inhibiting scents and replaced with a principled, righteous, charming, and optimistic spirit, discerning men will readily notice her, as he will, a physically attractive woman.

She's like a rare, delicate flower that a man, who possesses a right spirit, knows he must treat with the utmost respect and care. A man may truly grow leaps and bounds in the refreshing, titillating spirit she possesses, or either he won't be able to meet her high and honorable standards.

Because so many males have grown up with distorted concepts of themselves, women, and male-female relationships, their perception falls far short of males who have been reared with a proper perception of themselves, women and male-female relationships.

Consequently, males with distorted perceptions hardly make clear distinctions between women. All women have the same thing to offer, as far as they are concerned. Therefore, their quest for sexual conquest subjugates the more important virtues of a woman's spirit. Many men don't mature because they can't discern the very women who could enhance and fulfill them. Many of them lose good women because they are not smellin' themselves!

But what continues to amaze me are some women who have enhancing standards and characteristics, who lower their standards just to have a man. The same question that persists generation after generation is: Why do so many good women end up with not-so-good men? Even good men who are mentally, spiritually and intellectually compatible with those women can't figure this phenomena out!

I asked a young lady to tell me why this happens. She said she thinks there is some kind of mystique that a good female sees in the bad-boy image. There is a subtle attraction to experience forbidden fruit! Too many good women have lost more than they ever expected, once they got tangled up with the wrong male. When they got what they wanted, they lost what they had!

But the woman who stays the course, the woman who does right because it is right, the woman who thinks for herself and chooses wisely, has power - the power of influence! There are few things that can influence a man like a woman. When a woman is reared with, or at sometime in her life, acquires enhancing virtues, her power of influence is immeasurable .

In fact, King Solomon asks, "Who can find a virtuous woman? Her price is far above rubies." And then Solomon goes on to chronicle a woman's enhancing scents:

"Her man can trust her completely / she will do him good and not harm / she supplies her home with the necessary things / she chooses good foods / she rises early before sunrise in preparation for her day / she works energetically and keeps strong with vigorous exercise / she places the proper value on materials / sometimes she works late into the night completing projects / she sews and can make things with her hands / she is generous to the poor and helps the needy / she prepares her family for winter with proper clothing / her clothes are beautiful and in fine taste / her husband is respected because of her in the community

/ she has developed good entrepreneurial skills / she is respected in her own right in the community , and has an optimistic attitude toward life / her words are wisdom and she is kind to people / she is not lazy , and manages the business of her family / her children respect her and affirm her often / and her husband is always praising her. " [1]

To see a woman who is reared to reap the attributes of an enhancing spirit, or to find a woman who may not have had this advantage in her upbringing, but has chosen willingly to submit to the pruning process in her spirit, and then to conscientiously cultivate the type of spirit that produces these enhancing virtues, is a greater treasure for a man than for him to possess all the material accouterments in the world.

In reality, there is no substitute for the enhancing scents of a woman. Women who prioritize the acquisition of the virtues of an enhancing spirit in their male-female relationships, their value far exceeds rubies!

To be sure, enhancing scents are not as plentiful as inhibiting scents. Inhibiting scents come a dime-a-dozen. Inattention and carelessness are the grounds that breed them. Enhancing scents are like rare flowers. They take special attention and care to cultivate.

It is rare to find a woman whose delightful scents have been suitably and properly cultivated. Women who are inattentive and careless usually produce a crop of attitudes, a garden of tempers, and a harvest of disagreeable moods.

I want to introduce and present to some women, three scents that I have experienced, that enhance male-female relations. I know, because these are three that my mother possessed in my upbringing, and my wife possesses in our marriage and family: **Praise, intercession,** and **legacy.**

[1] Proverbs 31: 10-31

Praise

Flower: **Gesneraid**: The Gesneraid family is highly diverse, often very beautiful and amenable to both indoor and outdoor cultivation. They are among the most interesting and desirable of all horticultural and botanical subjects.

Scent: Gesneraids are classified according to the types of roots they have. Certain species have roots that are adapted for survival through periods of dormancy in response to climactic conditions such as drought or cold.

I'll never forget the day I was the guest speaker for "Singles Day" at a church. At one point in my presentation, I asked each person in the congregation to think how she or he began their day. I gave them a moment for reflection.

It is quintessential how we begin each day. I truly believe it makes a difference how an individual begins his or her day, no matter how challenging or rewarding the previous day was. Just as the adage says, "The first impression is a lasting impression." I also believe, our first act of each day sets the tone or the spirit that we will take into our day.

It is my belief that too many women are prisoners of the day before or the days before. Consequently, there is a lack of optimism, a lack of hope for the present day. This posture closes a woman's spirit and may prohibit her from receiving instruction, direction or correction from that day's defining moments.

There is counsel in the Scriptures on this very point. It admonishes "prisoners of the day" to relinquish your hold on your past by committing yourself to a fulfilling future.

"I am not all I should be but I am bringing all my ener-

gies to bear on this one thing: Forgetting the past and looking forward to what lies ahead." [1]

All that any of us have is today, and how a woman enters her todays can inhibit or enhance her spirit, and ultimately, her relationships with males. Therefore, *praise* is one of the best ways to begin each day. Praise raises the spirit!

Why praise? Because the human spirit is not static. Either it will be elevated or subjugated. Whatever thoughts, emotions or feelings a woman permits to dominate her spirit each day, will dictate the *scent* she will emanate to those around her. That scent either inhance or inhibit friendships.

Concerning men, more things tend to depress a woman's spirit than lift her spirit. It seems that negatives outnumber the positives. Someone says it takes more than one hundred muscles to frown, but only fourteen to smile. Unless a woman learns how to buoy her own spirit, she may be overcome by cynicism or depression.

But there is an antidote! Praise lifts your spirit like few activities can! Just think how your spirit soars when someone praises you for something you accomplished.

Praise is acknowledging that you choose to begin your day by giving honor to our Creator. The birds have sense enough to open their mouths early in the morning and give praise to the Creator. When a woman recognizes the power of praise, she will find it to be a daily requirement to fortify herself for whatever may be introduced into her day.

Praise is a personal decision to bring your spirit, soul and body into oneness with your Creator's will for that day. Not only does our Creator deserve acknowledgment and honor each day, our Creator also requires obedience. Obedience to the will of our Creator is the highest form of praise! Praise without obedience is nothing but lip-service.

[1] Philippians 3:13 (Living NT)

Let's bring it down to our human relationships. What good is it for me to sing or speak the praises of my mother and then disregard her loving requirements. My praise for her would be hollow and hypocritical. But when my obedience to her corresponds with my praise for her, she has received my highest regard.

Praise is like the opening of a flower in the morning to its Creator. Praise is the opening of our spirit to our Creator. Praise should be the first thing that comes out of the mouth of a woman in the morning, and the last thing before she goes to bed. Praise should be on her lips throughout the day.

A woman who seeks the recovery and restoration of her interrupted spirit accelerates her recovery as she learns how to praise our Creator daily. It is hard for a woman to praise our Creator for all the things she is thankful for and remain depressed in spirit. In fact, spirit-depression has a lot to do with the total absence of praise!

At first, I was undecided whether I would even use praise as an enhancing scent, surmising that some women would not understand the blessings and benefits and breakthrough that praise provides. But my personal experience of beginning each day with praise, and the blessings and benefits that I receive, was too compelling to omit it.

Praise is an antidote to complaining. You have to suspend one to commence with the other. I don't know anybody who enjoys being in the company of complainers. It's like some elders told us, "If you can't find something good to say, then don't say anything at all." Praise provides us with good things to say. There are so many things in life that we can be thankful for. People generally enjoy the company of those who have praiseworthy things to say.

Praise is a therapeutic, stress-reduction activity. When you count your blessings, your spirit calms and your stress decreases. If you don't believe me, try it. Open up your spirit and begin reciting to our Creator all that you are thankful for.

Praise is directed. The lavishing of praise has been given to many who don't deserve praise. What some people call praise is nothing but flattery. Some people worship position and prestige. They bathe certain people with flattery. But true praise is directed toward that which is praiseworthy. Read Philippians 4:8

Praise is one of the most enhancing scents a woman can release into the atmosphere of her male-female relationship. A woman who finds more to praise and thank our Creator for finds less to be depressed about. Her spirit cannot help but enhance her male-female relationships.

Finally, let me offer a few practical suggestions for women to keep the enhancing scent of praise fresh in your daily experience:

1. Read praise scriptures each morning. The book of Psalms is full of praise scriptures. It is even good to memorize certain passages that you can readily bring to the fore in time of need - that is - when you feel your spirit being interrupted. Here are some you can begin with:
Psalms 4; Psalms 8; Psalms 9; Psalms 11; Psalms 18; Psalms 23; Psalms 27; Psalms 30; Psalms 31; Psalms 34; Psalms 40; Psalms 42; Psalms 47; Psalms 54; Psalms 65; Psalms 66.

You can also find other praise readings that encourage your spirit in other sources. They may be proverbs, affirmations, stories, parables and poems.

2. Keep a praise journal. Jot down at least one thing that you are thankful for that day. Something that transpired that day that you want to chronicle and acknowledge to your Creator during your praise time. Keep your praise journal with you. You never know when you will get a revelation to write in your journal. Plus, if you don't write it at that time, you may not remember it later the way it was revealed to your spirit. Usually that first time, the phraseology is perfect. When you don't write it then, you may have a difficult time trying to word it in the exact same way.

Pull out your praise journal and read it whenever you feel your spirit being interrupted. And for those times that may not be apropos to refer to your journal, you can begin to praise our Creator in your spirit right where you are. All praise is not audible. Even if you are encountering opposition, you can silently praise the Creator in your spirit!

How often should you praise? As much as you need to praise! Praise until you get out of the habit of complaining. Praise until you stop speaking and thinking so negatively. Praise until people around you stop speaking so negatively in your presence. Praise until your attention is less preoccupied on your own problems and challenges, and more on others. Praise until it rubs off on the males who come into the sphere of your influence.

3. Find a praise partner. Your praise partner may be a female friend who needs encouragement and support. Or she may not be in the circle of your friends, but she has a need. She needs you. Introduce the praise partner concept to her. Let her know that you want her to be your praise partner.

At some time during the day, early morning before work, lunch break, evening phone call, you can share with each other a scripture, quotation, proverb or inspirational story that you have found that is uplifting, encouraging, and praiseworthy.

4. Affirmation as form of praise. Make it a habit to affirm some child, youth or adult each day. A spoken word, a card, a letter, or some kind of affirming expression may be a life saver for someone. It might simply be their beautiful smile, or their willingness to help someone in need. You can always find something to affirm someone for. Try it, you'll like it.

Praise is more than words or expressions. Praise is one of the most enhancing scents a woman can have. Women prune faster, heal quicker, and blossom better when they have a spirit of praise.

Intercession

Flower: **Daisy**: Known as a composite flower, the daisy is not a flower at all but a mass of clustering flowers called a head, so that the entire cluster resembles one single flower. or capitulum. The petals of the daisy are not single petals; they are fused petals and are a part of an entire, small, bilaterally symmetrical flower that is inserted at the rim of the head.

Scent: Composite flowers is the common name for one of the largest families of flowering plants, with more than 20,000 species. The common name refers to the clustering of the flowers into compact heads, so that the entire cluster resemble a single flower, as in the familiar Daisy. The daisy can be symbolic of Intercession. Intercession must be the spiritual tie that binds all women together as one. Oneness of spirit is the composite fragrance of sisterhood.

King Solomon said, "It is better for a man to dwell on the rooftop than in the house with a contentious woman."[1] Most men in male-female relationships would second the motion. Contention is an unhealthy spirit that pervades a home like a noxious odor! It is one of the most irritating scents that pervades many male-female relationships in particular, and relationships in general.

Let me start with relationships in general; particularly, female-to-female relationships. I have never witnessed contentions in a greater degree than females contending with each other. These are probably the most venomous contentions ever. I haven't seen men come close to the contentions

[1] Proverbs 21:9

that some females have with each other.

And don't let a group of females take sides against another group of females! Only war itself may be worst than the ongoing conflict that exists between the two female factions! I have never heard such explicit, graphic and degrading language that some females have used toward other females. Even some of their insidious tactics against each other have left me stunned to see what lengths women will go when in contention with other women.

I have been trying to figure out an antidote to this unfortunate phenomena for quite some time. What would it take for women who are saturated with the spirit of contention to prune this despicable formation from their spirit? My answer is that I truly don't know. But I think it is appropriate that something that is principled be tried.

When a disease or virus attacks a plant, there may be some uncertainty of the method or pesticide to use that will eliminate it, and not harm the plant at the same time. In the final analysis, to do nothing may mean the death of the flower. I went to my Compton's Interactive Encyclopedia for verification:

"There are more than 80,000 plant diseases known worldwide. In fact, all plants are vulnerable to attack by disease. Plant diseases are classified as noninfectious if they are caused by some environmental factor and are not transmitted from one plant to another. Infectious diseases are those that are caused by a diseased organism such as a virus."

"Viruses are common agents of infectious diseases in plants. When a virus enters a plant cell, it causes the cell to produce more viruses and often causes the death of the cell. The symptoms of viral disease vary. They often include malformation of stems and leaves, dead spots, or stunted growth... These viruses may cause further damage by

releasing toxic chemicals, or they may directly digest plant tissue."[2]

From this horticultural premise of the affects of diseases and viruses, we can see similar effects on women who are infected with the spirit of contention. Contention: 1) Can be transmitted to the spirit of another, 2) Causes formations on the character, dead spots (you figure that out), and stunts a woman's personal growth, 3) Releases toxic scents into a woman's relationships, 4) Can digest or eat away at a woman's effectiveness and influence, from the inside-out.

I hope you get my point. There needs to be a cessation of the bitterness, strife, and contention that is rife among women. Good friendships are lost. Wholesome relationships are severed, including mother-child relationships. Deeper still, one's own personal growth and development is stunted. Their toxic spirit pervades the atmosphere of their relationships. Contentiousness is more than an inhibiting spirit; it is a toxic spirit. When something is toxic, that means it is poisonous. Contention poisons relationships.

Contention also poisons male-female relationships. Most men have a serious problem with a mouthy woman, but when she is mouthy and contentious, some men are looking for the exit signs! Don't get me wrong. I am not saying that issues in male-female relationships should not be discussed or dealt with. They must. But I am referring to the spirit in which a woman discusses and deals with issues.

You might ask, "Well, what about men?" Men are not always at fault, or the ones who incite, instigate or contend. If the shoe fits a woman's foot, admit it. Anyway, this book is about the scents of a woman.

What is undeniable is that many women need to replace their inhibiting scent of contention, spite, revenge, and a

[2] Compton's Interactive Encyclopedia

host of other unhealthy and unclean spirits with an enhancing scent or spirit. I think I've found at least one antidote.

I read the section in the Compton's Interactive Encyclopedia subtitled, Disease Control. One option is to call a toxicologist. Toxicology is a science that deals with poisons and their effect and with the problems involved.

"Once a disease is established, the main approach to its control is eradication. Diseases may be eradicated by crop rotation - that is, a farmer may decide to replace a diseased crop with another species of crop plant. Sometimes a disease can be eradicated by pruning the diseased portion of the plant."[3]

I don't want you to think I am suggesting that men replace their contentious women as a remedy. That is not my call. What I recommend is pruning the diseased portion. Furthermore, I believe intercession is one remedy that may keep a contentious spirit away: Women interceding for women, and women interceding for their men.

When people are having problems and challenges, they don't need critics and judges; they need advocates, or intercessors.

The old African spiritual song says, "You can talk about me just as much as you please, but I'll talk about you, down on my knees!" Because intercession is a spiritual activity, one must have an inclination toward spirituality, or they will not use the medium of prayer for intercession.

Intercession, just like praise, is a spiritual activity. It is a positive, principled, enhancing activity of the spirit. Intercession is the continual act of presenting a person or a supplication before our Creator, that the Creator's will may be done. Intercession is usually carried on through the medium of prayer.

[3] Compton's Interactive Encyclopedia

As I said earlier, I don't have all the answers, especially for one of the most venomous states of being like a contentious spirit. I do know that for me, and for others who have tried it, intercession works. Intercession changes attitudes and feelings. **Intercession is part of the solution.**

Most people don't intercede or pray *for* people they don't like or in contention with. But most of them do have something to say *about* them. Since words are being used, they should be used as part of the solution.

I believe what makes the difference between pruning and growing or becoming more toxic in spirit and eventually hardened, is what we say and to whom we say it. When women resort to the spiritual activity of intercession and resist the unhealthy activity of gossiping and contention, a new growth begins. Should you have the inclination to say things to someone about someone that is not-so-positive, you can resist the temptation by incorporating a spirit of intercession. You can just say, "No comment," and then pray for them in your spirit.

When this becomes your practice, you will see how intercession is therapeutic, as well as a principled way of handling certain issues. Prayer changes things.

I would hasten to caution you that intercession is like seed planting. You are only responsible for creating a conducive atmosphere for that person or persons so that the seed may take root. You are not responsible for making them change, nor are you responsible for producing fruit.

All growth takes time. Our Creator is responsible for them changing and for harvesting the fruit of your intercession. Be careful not to expect immediate changes. You are just the sower, not the Reaper.

The enhancing scent (spirit) of intercession also creates a more conducive atmosphere in male-female relationships for positive and principled changes to take place. Hopefully, you can see that the atmosphere of contention only exacerbates the issues, but doesn't solve them.

I encourage you to begin pruning unhealthy and inhibiting growths and formations out of your spirit, and replace them with principled, spirit-enhancing activities. Consider starting with these suggestions:

1. List all the females that you may be in contention with. Do the same for males.

This includes all the females (past and present) with whom you have "issues," the females you don't like, females who have said or done something against you, females you have said or done something against them, and so on.

2. Identify and list all unhealthy scents that pervade your female-to-female relationships. Do the same for your male-female relationships.

It may include your daughter, mother, sister, female co-workers, husband, former spouse, son, brother, male co-workers, etc. Even as trivial as your feelings or emotions toward them may seem, list them. Be honest.

3. List the names of those females that you will intercede for regularly. Do the same for males.

There are probably more principled ways to prune and/or eliminate the inhibiting scents of a woman. A contentious spirit is only one of many lingering scents that virtually destroy female-to-female, as well as, male-female relationships.

Intercession is an excellent replacement for a contentious, bitter, revengeful, pungent spirit. It's better than being replaced by another woman, especially if you have a good man.

Legacy

Flower: **Perennial**: Perennials are present in all seasons of the year. Adjectives that describe perennials are, persistent, enduring, and constant. Perennials normally live for many years and best adapted to a broad range of growing conditions. Many perennials are seldom bothered by insects and disease. Perennials are regularly repeated and renewed.

Scent: There are over 1000 different perennials with their diverse attributes (scents). Here are a few: *Bee Balm*: Minty fragrance. *Carolina Lupine*: Drought tolerant. *Crane's Bill*: Nearly indestructible. *Lady's Mantle*: Beautiful foliage. *Daylily*: Withstands neglect.

The last, but certainly not the least, enhancing scent of a woman that I will address is *legacy*. Why legacy? Because women are seed bearers, blessed by our Creator to pass on their legacy to and through their seed.

The general definition of legacy is, "something handed down from an ancestor or predecessor, or from the past." But more specifically, **I define legacy as, a calculated, studied, and predetermined resolve to confer upon a chosen successor, noble traits of character. In short, legacy is producing fruit.**

Just as a plant or tree produces fruit, so the legacy of life is to produce fruit, as directed by our Creator to humanity's first parents: "Be fruitful and multiply."[1]

When a woman lives a life for her own self-indulgence and selfish interests, she has not truly lived; she merely exists. She may possess all the outer trappings of life, but

[1] Genesis 1:28

if she bears no noble legacy, she is empty indeed.

I went home to Youngstown, Ohio some years ago for a holiday. We were looking at television and some special was on about Queen Elizabeth of England (Prince Charles' mother). They talked about her substantial wealth and the accouterments of life that she enjoyed - servants, cooks, chauffeurs, personal attendants and bodyguards. I'll never forget the comment my mother made. She said, "If the Queen would make her own bed, she would be a better woman." Her children will inherit her wealth but that does not mean she will leave them an honorable legacy.

You do not have to achieve national or international prominence or recognition to impart a legacy. *Your daily life from this day forward can become your legacy.* To rise from a weighted, wounded, oppressed or violated spirit to bear our Creator's fruit of the Spirit - love, joy, peace, patience, gentleness, goodness, faith, meekness and self control - is a legacy to all who come into the sphere of your influence. When children, youth and adults can come into your presence and bear witness to your restored spirit and life, that's legacy!

My mother's legacy of living, loving and parenting is rare. There are many honorable character traits that my mother possesses that has enhanced my life and relationships. My mother lives what she professes, and professes what she lives. She is one of the most spiritually-balanced persons, with a great sense of humor, wise and one of the most giving women you will ever meet. But the legacy she bestows was honed on the anvil of struggle and pain.

My mother is not a stranger to a weighted, wounded, oppressed or violated spirit. Some of the experiences she encountered and endured have caused women to become bitter. Without one complaint, she used them as stepping stones. She did not permit them to deter her, because she had committed herself to bestowing her legacy on her children.

The predominant legacy that each of my mother's children received is probably different. I never asked my two sisters or my brother what legacy they received from mommy. That ought to make good conversation at one of our family get-togethers. All I can tell you about is the legacy I have received from her that I have chosen to give to my children.

My mother came from very humble beginnings. She was born in Selma, Alabama. But oftentimes, sacrifice is the foundation of legacy. Some who have made the greatest of sacrifice have left behind the greatest legacy. At a young age, her family, which included her mother, two brothers and four sisters, moved north to Ohio.

My mother worked (and still works) as a domestic worker. That's menial labor in some people's limited view, but I call my mother a master artist. I have watched her go into some of the dirtiest homes and transform them into masterpieces! She helped put my two sisters and my brother through college by transforming homes!

My mother has a signature on her work that is not duplicated! She has passed on her imprimatur to all her children. We have an excellent work ethic, and if someone gives us a responsibility, it will be done right, the first time, and in such a way that our signature will be distinct. That's a legacy within itself, but that's not my predominant legacy.

My mother did something that surprised us all. She went to night school and got her high school diploma, while working during the day cleaning homes and offices. Her legacy of transcending obstacles is securely riveted in my mind. But although it is a legacy that I retain, it's not my predominant legacy.

I have witnessed my mother standing alone many times. She is a lover of the truth. Once she understands what is truth, she will not be moved. In this life, most people are "hearers, but not doers of the truth." When one stands for truth, oftentimes, you have to stand alone. My mother was periodically "attacked" for the truth she stood for. Some people to this day don't like my mother because of her truth stances. She has bequeath her love of the truth to me. I too have had to stand alone at times.

Being a lover of the truth can be a lonely road. Not many people travel it, so my mother was not surrounded by a lot of people. By that, I mean, she wasn't real popular, but you'd better believe, she was respected to the highest!

Well, fruit don't fall too far from the tree. The same thing goes for her four children. But we prefer respect over popularity any day. The love of the truth, and being willing to deal with the consequences for standing for truth is a legacy she passed down to me. But that still is not my predominant legacy.

The predominant legacy that I graciously received from my mother, and have made a calculated, studied, and predetermined resolve to confer on my daughters is, *precept* and *example*. Out of all my mother's legacies, precept and example rises above them all! MY MOTHER LIVED HER LEGACY!

In my first book, *Rearing African Children Under American Occupation*, I dedicated it to my mother. I penned these words of dedication: **"To my mother, Beatrice. It's all your fault! I am eternally thankful to you for giving me your love of the Truth, your powerful living example of parenting, and how to preserve one's dignity and integrity when standing for principle amid opposition."**

I cannot begin to tell you all of what my mother had to

endure, even in her marital relationship. All I will tell you was that her spirit has been weighted, wounded, oppressed and violated. Some things I didn't find out until I was married and had a family. But it was her precept and example that rose above the fray and impacted my life so profoundly that I grew up with no mental or emotional scars! I carried no baggage from my upbringing into adulthood or marriage. What a legacy!

Of all she suffered in spirit, soul and body, I never once heard her complain. All that she experienced and encountered, I was never the recipient of any transference. She bore it patiently as long as she could and with dignity, principle and resolve, because she had a higher objective in mind: **She wanted to honor her Creator's spirit by living rightly before her children by precept and example. And she did!**

Precept is defined as, "a rule or principle, a standard of action or conduct." Example is defined as, "something worthy of imitation, a model." My mother's precept and example is my main legacy worth passing on to my daughters.

Of course, my wife and I are rearing our daughters to have a good work ethic, to love the truth and be willing to deal with the consequences, both positive and negative, for standing for truth. We want them not to think it strange to have to stand alone at times, or be "attacked" for their truth stances. And they can stand, like their grandmother, with a poise and dignity rarely seen in in our modern society.

But it is my calculated, studied, and predetermined resolve to confer a legacy of precept and example by my life, just as my mother lived before me. There is nothing more powerful than to live a righteous and principled life. This gives meaning and power to our words.

It's like a poem I read that began: "I'd rather see a sermon than to hear one any day." That's the kind of fruit that my daughters and those who come into the sphere of my influence can benefit from, at any time and in any place.

Now that I have finished waxing nostalgic, I want to ask you a question: What legacy do you have to bestow? I'm not asking what you want to be remembered for, but what legacy do you have to bestow? And the rhetorical question is: Who will you bestow your legacy upon?

A noble legacy bestowed is an enhancing scent that can transcend generations. A calculated, studied, and predetermined resolve to confer a legacy can determine how a woman responds in her male-female relationship. Legacy is akin to purpose. When a woman knows the legacy she is to pass on, she will discern anyone or anything that contradicts it. She must then govern herself accordingly.

Passing on a noble legacy may mean deferred gratification. But gratification is relative and conditional. But there are few things more fulfilling than for a woman to see her noble legacy live on in someone blessed by our Creator with her legacy.

All praise to our Creator that my mother has lived to see the fruit of her legacy! You can tell she's about to burst when her grandchildren visit her in Ohio. My mother is able to see her grandchildren beginning to reflect the fruit of her legacy.

My mother is so proud of me! And when she reads my books, she says, "Where did you get this wisdom from? How do you know so much about women, being a man?" I just smile and say, "It's all your fault!"

And then for me to be married to a woman whose parents have rightly and meticulously sown, pollinated and cultivated their daughter in such a spiritual and principled way, I am blessed among men!

My wife also has a calculated, studied, and predetermined resolve to confer the legacy she has received from her wise mother. Although my wife has quite a few choices, if her legacy is simply to prepare her daughters to be the woman and wife her mother prepared her to be, then the men who marry my daughters will experience what I have for the past eighteen years - heaven on earth!

There is power in inculcating our Creator's natural principles into parenting methodology: If a father and mother would place their full and undivided attention on sowing, pollinating, cultivating and conferring a noble legacy on their children instead of focusing on their own individual happiness, the enhancing scents from their home would permeate their whole neighborhood!

Finally, I believe that conferring a legacy is also important for single women. *Legacy is really a giving-back to someone for a specific purpose*. I am excited when I see single women and men giving back to their communities. Many single women take the initiative to volunteer in all sorts of wholesome community endeavors, and they are all to be commended. We need so many more single women to do the same.

Yet, there is a deeper contemplation I want single women to peruse in deciding what legacy they will confer. What did you need as a child or youth? What essentials were omitted in your upbringing that you needed conferred on you that no child or youth should be without? It might be that very thing that you will have to give back as your legacy to a child or youth in the sphere of your influence.

The African American spiritual says it best: "If I can help somebody as I pass along. If I can cheer somebody with a word or song. If I can show somebody [she] is traveling wrong, then my living shall not be in vain."

Think for a moment of all the women who have left their legacy with you. A mother, grandmother, or an aunt. Maybe it was a woman teacher, a neighbor or a woman who befriended you. Bath yourself in the warmth, strength and fragrance of her spirit. Do you remember her words of encouragement? Her quiet strength while under pressure? Her gentle, loving touch that said, "I understand," without her saying a word?

What's her name? Is she still alive? Then send her a card, call her, write her, visit her, send her flowers - just tell her - how much her legacy has meant to you. Let her know that her words of encouragement, her wisdom, her example, her letters, her love, has buoyed you up on the perplexing sea of life. **Now go and do likewise!**

May the aromatic and pervasive scent of the legacy our Creator blesses you to impart remain an ever-fresh scent in the spirit, mind and life of some girl, some lady, even your daughter.

A Call To The Village Women

As I observe this new crop of females, I'm fascinated, frightened and frustrated. As I witness the disconcerting experiences so many young females endure today, I am *fascinated* how many of them still function reasonably well. I was talking to a female friend of my family about the plight of many young females. I remarked, "You older women could not survive what a lot of these young girls are going through today. You would have probably gone crazy a long time ago." She agreed with me.

So much "stuff" - for lack a better word - has converged on this generation of young females that was not so visibly present when I was growing up. To put it mildly, these young females have problems! Serious personal problems, male-female problems, family problems, and a whole lot more problems!

It's *frightening* to see how so many females are becoming casualties at such a young age, casualties of degradation, destruction and death. The statistics continue to spiral astronomically, as more and more young females lose their way.

I was surfing the Internet, looking for some statistics that pertained to youth. I hit the site of the Joint Center for Political and Economic Studies, based in Washington, D.C. The youth statistics on homicides, suicides, AIDS and HIV, sexually transmitted diseases, etc., were frightening. In particular, all the statistics on young females are on the increase.

Of course, the primary "at-risk" group is said to be females of color, but we know better. Alcohol, tobacco and drug usage, sexually transmitted diseases, rape and brutal beatings - to name a few - are equal opportunity destroyers! They don't discriminate, they denigrate, humiliate and annihilate females, at will. Offering help and hope is not a so-called race issue. It is an issue of concern, compassion, and caring for one another.

It's not my intention to sound like a dooms-day prophet, nor am I a pessimist. I am just telling a painful truth about the reality of some of our daughters, nieces, female cousins and neighbors.

I believe the optimism of youth is being eclipsed by the ominous consequences of not only their choices and decisions, but more so, the conditions that adults have created in our homes and society in which youth must make their choices and decisions within - in short - shared responsibility and accountability.

It's also frustrating as I analyze and synthesize the young female predicament, for two reasons. *First, it's frustrating because it's hard to get many of these young girls to slow down.* Some young girls out there are fourteen and fifteen years-old, looking like they're twenty-two, and trying to act like it! And the guys are taking advantage of them!

When relatives and friends, who are concerned try to counsel, caution or correct these young girls, some of them get upset. And the disrespect that some of them have toward their parents or elders, would not have been tolerated a generation ago! Although I'm not in agreement with some of the methods that were used back then, at least the intentions were right.

Secondly, some of these young girls are partaking in some of the most repulsive, degrading lifestyles imaginable. *It's frustrating trying to elicit help to save them from the ravaging wolves of society.* Although there are a few sincere and unbiased groups and individuals helping young females, many of the women of the village remain distanced and silent, except when criticizing these young girls.

One of the most poignant examples was given by Dr. Martin King, Jr., in his sermon about the Good Samaritan. Dr. King recited the story of how a man had been badly beaten and robbed and was left by the side of the road to die. First, the priest and then the Levite came by, looked at him, and continued on their way. They would become ceremonially unclean if they touched the victim. In addition to that excuse, Dr. King surmised that the priest and Levite thought, "If I stop, what will happen to me?" Maybe the robbers were lurking near. So they went on without aiding the victim.

But the Samaritan, one who was looked upon as an outcast by the priest and Levite, came where the wounded man was, cleaned him up, put oil on his wounds, put the victim on his donkey, took him to an inn, and paid for his recuperation. Dr. King, commenting about the Samaritan, said, the Samaritan did not think, "If I stop, what will happen to me?" He probably thought, "If I don't stop and help this man, what will happen to him?"

These are my questions to the women of the village: *Are you your sister's keeper?* Or have you gotten too busy, too burdened, or too bourgeois, to offer help and hope to these troubled, young sisters? If you don't take the time to help, what will happen to them?

If you don't stop and assist these young, problem-oriented females, what will happen to them? If you don't take the time to bring your knowledge, expertise, skills and resources to the fore - intervention - if you will, how many more casualties will there be among them?

To add insult to injury, so many young females today are gullible and vulnerable. It's a totally different exploited and explicit genre that they are operating in. I call it, the "Ricki Lake Syndrome!" Where is their shame? Where is their self respect? What is happening that a partial segment of young females can't discern that the media and their cronies are exploiting them for entertainment and profit!

We are not even talking about "scents" of a woman, as it pertains to the Ricki Lake Syndrome. These young females are giving off fumes, and these fumes are toxic! Some think that this culturally diverse group of females are irrecoverable. I disagree. Many of them just don't know the full extent of the consequences of their choices and decisions. I also believe that many of them want a principled, positive change in their lives, but they don't have the faintest idea where to start, or who will help them.

Here's my burden, and the reason I am making a call to the village women: Too many women remain uncommitted to becoming part of the solution.

It is quite obvious that most males are limited in their understanding of spirit. Although they have resources they can and must bring to bear to assist these young girls, they are still limited. It is the interrupted spirit of these young girls that need restoration and recovery. They have been weighted, wounded, oppressed or violated.

Most females connect in spirit first. When there is a kindred spirit among two or more females, they usually take the time and opportunity to communicate, disseminate vital information and instruction, share, even their clothing, and solve problems.

Most females do more *for* males than they do *with* males. But most females do more *with* females than they do *for* females. These challenged young females need other females to do things *with* them, not *for* them. They need the women of the village to connect with them in spirit. Once this is done, they are usually open to communicate, receive vital information and instruction, and work on resolving their challenges. But they cannot do it by themselves.

I am making a call to the village women to find a troubled or challenged female girl or youth and personalize her. Get in her space! Each one, reach one. You don't have to look any farther than your own community.

Some of you women who are reading this right now, know that it took a certain person to help you through your problems until you blossomed into the woman you are today. You can bear witness to the spirit of intercession.

Let me give a brief overview of some of the immediate needs that the village women can attend to with many young females. Every female needs a **mentor**. When I was growing up, we didn't call them mentors; they were examples. We had the privilege of hearing and seeing them in our churches, schools and communities. They exemplified how we should govern ourselves as young men and young women.

Today's females and males, not only need observation, they need hands-on attention. Mentoring is one solution. I offer a different slant to traditional mentoring. I have seen a lot of well-meaning adults volunteer to mentor, but their spirit did not connect with that young person. Although it's not guaranteed, it is better when the spirit of the young person and the adult connects.

But beyond that, I suggest that you find a child to mentor who wants to aspire to the same profession or vocation that you have. For example, my youngest daughter wants to be a veterinarian. She's had a vet as a mentor since she was six. She's fourteen now. By the time she matriculates, probably at Tuskegee University, which has one of the best vet schools in the country, she will be well advanced.

Even if you don't find a young female who wants a career in your field, you can still mentor. Mentoring is personalizing, encouraging and providing help and hope. All it takes is a young girl and some time. I am calling the village women to mentor.

As you have read, this book is dedicated to the women of Emmanuel-Brinklow. That is a church in Brinklow, Maryland. The Women's Ministries department has been sponsoring a Cotillion for several years. Their primary focus is to assist high school seniors in raising funds to attend college. High school juniors are also included.

Throughout the year, up until the Cotillion, they provide a diversity of seminars, workshops, culturally-enriching experiences, and community service events. Not only does it reap financial rewards, it also enhances their interpersonal, socialization, and entrepreneurial skills.

I am calling the village women, especially those who are connected with a religious or social organization, to sponsor **cotillions** for young females. I would even encourage some of you to take some cotillions into the inner cities! I'm serious. There are many young, gifted females in the inner city, for whatever reason, who lack the exposure to these information-oriented, life-enhancing functions. Hopefully, it can become a yearly event.

There is an all-out attack on the public school system. It mostly comes from partisan battlefronts with ulterior motives. Some want to divert public tax money into private and religious schools, while leaving the public schools to fend for the crumbs that fall off the table. This is wrong. As long as we pay taxes, we ought to make our public schools acceptable and accountable. Therefore, I am calling the village women to **adopt-a-school**. Some of you work in corporations who would underwrite this kind of community endeavor. Some businesses are already doing it, but there needs to be more.

There are many women who are in position to help provide human and material resources to schools who are lacking. Getting a needs assessment from the principal can get you up and rolling. What is needed is your influence and involvement to bring fledgling schools up to standard.

There are blatant disparities in public school funding. The more opulent districts, who have a substantial tax base, lack very little, as it pertains to human and material resources. In addition to your influence and involvement, your **advocacy** for struggling schools and school children is essential. The time for criticizing is over. Your help is needed.

While I am on the topic of school, I am calling the village women to become **tutors**. There are tutorial programs in our communities already in existence. You can assist them, or you can identify a girl and tutor on your own time. Either way, a young female is receiving help and hope from a concerned and committed woman of the village.

I am finding that at the time of female adolescence, there are very few *structured programs* for them. By structured programs, I am referring to ongoing programs. At the time when their hormones are kicking in, there is an absence of structured programs as a support system for families and communities in need.

One of the most successful and increasingly popular programs in the African American community is a **Rites of Passage**. This program assists young girls in a girlhood-to-womanhood transition. This wholistic program addresses the physical, mental-emotional, spiritual, social, cultural, and economic growth and development of the female. But there are not nearly enough Rites of Passage programs, nor is there enough adult participation. There should not be a church or community center without a Female Rites of Passage and a Male Rites of Passage program. I am making a call to the village women to become a part of Rites of Passage or wholesome, structured programs that enhance and develop young females toward principled living.

Mentoring, cotillions, adopt-a-school, advocacy, tutoring, Rites of Passage - structured programs - are just a few, but not limited to, the way women of the village can become actively involved in the lives of young females.

You can start a drama club, organize or enroll a young female in a writers guild, initiate a sewing club, sponsor them in a performing arts summer camp, or a summer math and science camp. It all depends upon your abilities, resources and contacts. But do something. Each woman of the village needs to reach one young female in a substantive way.

If you are not frightened and frustrated as you witness the tragic plight of so many young females, you should pinch yourself. If you don't have a burden or desire to positively intervene in the life of at least one young female, what will happen to her?

Just for a moment, put yourself in their four inch platform shoes. Imagine yourself being exploited by the media, victimized by misogynist lyrics, abused by males, no employable skills, hardheaded, living in the fast lane, and oblivious to the consequences of your choices and lifestyle - and you're just sixteen years old, or younger!

Furthermore, most of you know where these young females are headed; to a multiplicity of bad experiences with the opposite sex. They don't need to go where many of you have come from. They don't need to experience the hurt, pain and unfulfillment of looking for love in all the wrong places. We don't need any more prodigal daughters! We don't need any more missing daughters posted on the side of milk cartons!

Will you just walk by these troubled young females (some are struggling mothers) without offering help and hope? It only takes a little planning and a lot of follow-through. If you are already actively involved, then recruit other village women to help. If you are not sure what you can or want to do, pray about it, find a need, and fill it. After all, you are your sister's keeper.

Redefining Moments

A sower was on the way to the flower garden when some seeds fell out of his bag, among the weeds. Shortly thereafter, these seeds sprouted. To their surprise, the adult weeds that surrounded them made fun of them, laughed at them, hit them, and called them ugly names. Some weeds refused to acknowledge them.

All the flowers could do was huddle together in fear and uncertainty. They could not figure out why they were being hit, mistreated, abused and ignored. As you can imagine, as the years went by, the flowers began to think negatively of themselves. Bitterness, fear, and even depression set into their petals. They would even lash out at each other at times.

The flowers also hated their home. It was a disheartening atmosphere, but they were stuck. Who would feed them? A few of the flowers talked about running away. Some did. Other flowers couldn't wait to get old enough to leave.

Some of the male weeds began to mess with some of the young flowers. They would touch their petals and stems in inappropriate ways. Then they would threaten to hurt them if they told. The violated flowers felt so guilty and unclean.

There were flowers who could never do anything right. No matter how hard they tried, they could never measure up to adult weed's rigid standards. It was never good enough. The flowers blamed themselves.

Many times, the flowers just needed a hug and a word of encouragement, but some of the adult weeds refused them. Sometimes, the flowers wanted to talk and ask questions about so many things. But some adult weeds never took the time. They were either too busy or unconcerned.

What was astounding to the flowers was that many of the

adult weeds went to church. They seemed to be so different, so religious, so kind, there, but when they got home, they were back to their mean selves.

Some of the flowers were never trusted by the adult weeds. They hardly could go out or make friends. They couldn't engage in much of the innocent activities that the other weeds were allowed. They felt like Cinderella and Old Maids. Their future seemed dismal.

One day, the sower's daughter was walking along. She looked down and saw the most beautiful bouquet of flowers sitting among the weeds. She lavished them with words they had never heard growing up. She carefully uprooted them and took them home. She watered them and nourished them with good flower food.

At home, she put them in some warm, dark, earth. It felt so good. Every day, she talked to them in a sweet-sounding voice, telling them how beautiful and special they were. She told them that the Creator had made them for a special purpose and how they were meant to bring joy, comfort, and gladness to the lives of many, becoming one of the most precious and treasured gifts that could ever be given.

Understanding their purpose for the first time, their drooping petals began to sit upright. For too long, they thought they were weeds, consigned to the life of a weed. But now, they found out they weren't what they had been told.

Now, the flowers had to prepare for their special purpose. Even though they wished that they had been prepared as a child, they decided not to dwell on their past.

The flowers also knew that they had to let go of their bitterness, anger, hatred and depression. Some flowers had developed growths and formations on them that caused them physical and emotional problems, but the sower's daughter called a toxicologist and she examined them. She said that the growths had to be removed immediately, if they were to fulfill their purpose given them by the Creator. But that would be an individual decision.

Some of the flowers became fearful. It wasn't that they didn't want the growths and formations removed, they were just afraid of the process for removing them. They knew that their painful past would have to be delved into, which many of the flowers were trying to forget. Some flowers were willing; some flowers resisted pruning.

The sower's daughter sat down and had a heart-to-heart talk with the flowers. She said, "When I was walking through the woods, I didn't see you at first. It was your scent that attracted me. And then when I saw you, I could not believe that such a hideous smell was coming from such beautiful flowers." It was then, that they divulged to her their past abuse, neglect, mistreatment, beatings, molestations and rapes, and a host of other indignities.

It was not until they met her and learned about the Creator's special purpose for them, that they had glimmers of hope for their future. But even with this knowledge, the flowers still had an unpleasant scent, though not as strong as before. The sower's daughter asked, "Do you want your scent to be as beautiful as you are? If so, you will have to submit to the pruning knife. At times, it will hurt, but just think of what you will become, and you will get through it all right."

All the flowers vowed to support each other. They would intercede for each other daily. They would call, send cards, and encourage each other instead of gossiping, criticizing, and complaining. They knew that restoration and recovery of their true scent may take a little longer with some than others, but they all committed to go the distance. They all began the pruning process. They wanted to bring closure to their past, and a blossoming of their future.

Once they submitted to the pruning process, they discovered other flowers they didn't know who were also going through it, too. They lent their support and encouragement. Sometimes, they met together and fellowshipped, talked about their pruning experiences, and bonded for life.

Soon, people began to notice changes in the flowers. They were not as unforgiving, fearful and depressed like they used to be. Their scents, which they had gotten used to, but did not realize how nauseating and unpleasant to be around, were dissipating, and being replaced with a pleasant aroma. Male flowers were coming out of the woodwork!

Realizing their positive changes, the flowers began to praise their Creator daily! They knew that other troubled flowers needed them, even the weeds that mistreated, misunderstood, and misquoted them. Intercession became their way of responding to them.

There was one more surprise. The sower's daughter was getting married, and guess who she chose as her bouquet? Imagine that! The flowers that had grown up among the weeds, hampered with bad scents and the life-threatening growths and formations, now became the most beautiful, sweet-smelling flowers around! The bouquet of flowers cheered, cried, hugged, sang, and praised their Creator! And when the bride walked down the aisle with them, their mellifluous scents filled the air!

As the bouquet of flowers left the wedding, they saw some young drooping female flowers standing by the side of the road; their growths and formations were already visible. The beautiful, sweet-smelling bouquet went over, embraced them, and said, "Let's talk." It was their redefining moment!

My Tribute

Women have so many things to celebrate! You are the most beautiful creation ever. Your beauty is unequalled in all of creation. What a sight for a man to behold! Only our Creator's mind and hands could have conceived and formed you. You have been given the blessed gift of procreation. The miracle of childbirth attests to our Creator's trust in you. What a privilege! Your motherly-comforting nature has been a haven for bleeding knees and hurt feelings of untold children. The safest place on earth to a child is a mother's lap. Your sixth sense - intuition - endowed upon you by our Creator, has been your early warning system that has predicted and prohibited a multitude of events, before they happened. Men have yet to appreciate and appropriate this special gift. Your hands are blessed and indispensible. They have calmed, encouraged and are always creating something out of nothing. Your touch is stimulating, soothing, and sensitive. Blessed and indispensible are your hands. Your strength hides in the reservoir of your femininity until it is summoned. You have carried the greatest burdens of the human family on your back, and you have yet to weaken. What amazing strength you have shown the universe. Your feminine mystique never fails to interest men. It is like a captivating scent that draws a man to its source.
Your eyes penetrate the human facade and perceive the real spirit of a man. You need no words. Your eyes say it all.
You are the perfect companion and completion of man. That's how our Creator fashioned you. Man may say he was created first, but he can never say he was complete without you. Women have so many things to celebrate!

Other Books by Kwame Ronnie Vanderhorst

****

* Rearing African Children Under American Occupation

* Family Matters: Hope & Healing

* Smellin' Ourselves: What Men Need To Understand About Our Women